THE COCAINE PRINCESS 9

King Rio

**Lock Down Publications and Ca$h
Presents**
The Cocaine Princess 9
A Novel by *King Rio*

King Rio

Lock Down Publications
P.O. Box 944
Stockbridge, Ga 30281
www.lockdownpublications.com

Copyright 2023 by King Rio
The Cocaine Princess 9

Lock Down Publications
Like our page on Facebook: Lock Down Publications @
www.facebook.com/lockdownpublications.ldp
Book interior design by: **Shawn Walker**

Stay Connected with Us!

Text **LOCKDOWN** to 22828 to stay up-to-date with new releases, sneak peaks, contests and more…

Thank you!

Submission Guideline.

Submit the first three chapters of your completed manuscript to ldpsubmissions@gmail.com, subject line: Your book's title. The manuscript must be in a .doc file and sent as an attachment. Document should be in Times New Roman, double spaced and in size 12 font. Also, provide your synopsis and full contact information. If sending multiple submissions, they must each be in a separate email.

Have a story but no way to send it electronically? You can still submit to LDP/Ca$h Presents. Send in the first three chapters, written or typed, of your completed manuscript to:

LDP: Submissions Dept
P.O. Box 944
Stockbridge, Ga 30281

DO NOT send original manuscript. Must be a duplicate.

Provide your synopsis and a cover letter containing your full contact information.

Thanks for considering LDP and Ca$h Presents.

Dedication

In loving memory of Angela "Angie" Rabotte.

King Rio

Prologue

It was 10:17 on the morning of her 23rd birthday, April 21st, 2015, when Alexus Costilla came out of the medically induced coma.

Rita Mae Bishop, her mother, was sitting in an easy chair next to her bed, so busy reading the Bible that she didn't realize Alexus's eyes had opened.

There was a powerfully-built white man standing under the wall-mounted television across from her bed. He wore slacks and a navy blue blazer with FBI stenciled over the left breast in big yellow letters.

Two more FBI agents were standing at the big wooden door at the entrance of her hospital room.

She tried to remember how she'd gotten here and couldn't think of a thing. Her last memory was an argument with her husband, Blake "Bulletface" King, a rapper whose name was synonymous with Jay Z and Lil Wayne. He had put his gun to her sister Mercedes's head with the intent to shoot her dead for allegedly setting him up, and Alexus had pulled her own gun on him to save her sister.

She remembered seeing Blake leave, but nothing else came to mind.

"Alexus!" Rita shouted excitedly when she saw that Alexus was awake.

Alexus tried to voice a reply but all that came out was a hoarse whisper: "Where... Blake..."

"Sshhh." Rita walked to the bedside, lifted Alexus's hand in hers, and pressed her lips to her daughter's forehead. "You've got a tube down your throat. Relax. Blake just left with Meach and Biggs. He's got a show in Chicago he has to make it to. Enrique is out in the waiting area with Pedro."

Alexus felt weak. Weak and heavily sedated. She looked at her left arm and saw stitches in several different places. Her left leg and foot were bandaged. She moved her right arm and heard a metallic clink.

Her wrist was handcuffed to the bedrail.

"Sit still, baby," Rita said. "Just sit still. The Lord has you wrapped in his arms."

"Blake..."

"Hold on, I'll call him." Rita dialed a number on her smartphone and put it on speakerphone.

"What's up, Momma." Blake's voice calmed Alexus instantly.

"Alexus just woke up. Talk. She can hear you."

Blake paused; then, "I love you, baby."

Alexus smiled.

"I'm on my way back to the airport now," he continued. "I was about to get on the jet and fly to Chicago. I got a concert out there tonight. Be strong, okay? They'll probably be taking you to jail but don't worry, we'll get you right out. The judge gave you a forty-million-dollar bond. They indicted almost everybody right after the suicide bombing. Britney will get the bond paid and you'll be home asap."

Alexus managed to utter one final word: "Mexico."

Both Rita and Blake understood what she meant.

Alexus Costilla was the boss of the Costilla Cartel, a Mexican drug cartel that now included every major cartel in Mexico.

She wanted to go to Mexico, where her family had ruled for years, and where she was now considered the ultimate queen of the drug trade.

Chapter 1

Three hours and forty million dollars later Alexus Costilla left the Los Angeles courthouse in a wheelchair that was made of 24-karat gold and encrusted with white diamonds. Knowing her taste for the finer things in life, Enrique had paid top dollar for the customized wheelchair weeks earlier, shortly after the suicide bombing that had hospitalized her and her sister and cost Enrique his left hand.

Alexus's sparkling fleet of seven snow white Rolls-Royce Phantoms were parked at the curb. News correspondents from every major television network were waiting out front with cameras and microphones, and they immediately began shouting questions.

"Alexus, what do you have to say about the charges being brought against you?"

"Are you really a cartel boss, as the indictments allege?"

"Is it true that you and Bulletface have called it quits?"

"If you two get divorced, will you share custody of both children?"

"Have you heard about the new kid?"

"How has the news of your uncle Flako's death affected you?"

Alexus had no comment. Her attorney, Britney Bostic, waved the reporters off.

As soon as Alexus and her mother were situated in the backseat of one of the Phantoms, her driver headed straight for the airport.

The now-removed feeding tubes that had been her source of food for the past month and a half had Alexus's throat sore. She sipped half mouthfuls of water at a time and winced with every swallow. Her stitches itched. The burns on her leg itched.

"Everything's fine," Rita kept saying.

Alexus just stared out her window and sipped more water. She was in pain. Her left wrist had been lacerated and broken in the explosion. She had a hundred and forty-seven stitches and fifty-three staples in her body, and third-degree burns on her left leg.

It would be a long recovery, she knew. One that would be painful and difficult but certainly possible.

"Blake's in charge of everything now," Enrique said from the passenger seat as he lowered his window a crack and put fire to the end of a Cuban cigar. "He's handling it all pretty well. Made you another $180 million already. He's like that Big Meach guy we used to deal with, only ten times wealthier. Our product has taken over most of the country. He's even nudging his way into Colorado's legal marijuana market with four shops opening there in the coming months. Some guy named Glo shot at him about a week ago in Chicago, and he went through hell dealing with Gamuza in LA, but he's doing great. He just sent me a text saying he's waiting to see you at the airport."

"Forget Blake," Alexus said. "He keeps fucking cheating on me."

Rita nodded her head. She had her trusty old Bible peeking out of the black leather Birkin bag on the lap of her black Prada sundress. Fifty carats of refulgent white diamonds were shining in the custom designed Chanel tennis bracelet on her left wrist. She too had burns, old burns on the left side of her face from when Alexus's aunt Jenny Costilla had detonated a bomb on her front porch, but the scarred tissue was unnoticeable beneath her makeup. Her hair was done in a short, neat bob. Her piercing brown eyes worriedly studied Alexus, while Alexus continued to gaze thoughtfully out her window, seemingly unfazed by all that was going on.

"Aren't you upset?" Rita asked. "Hurt? Anything? You look like you're at peace when clearly peace is not what we're experiencing. And now Blake's been sleeping with some ratchet stripper girl from Atlanta. Her name's Barbie. You cannot be at ease. I'm here, baby. I know you're grown and all but you'll always be my baby. Talk to me."

Alexus took a brief moment to reply; the news of Blake cheating again momentarily stopped her breath. "Just get me to Mexico," she said finally, fighting back a flood of tears. "I'm done with him, anyway. He pulled a gun on my sister. I'll let him keep running the cartel. Let him give all the orders and deal with the savages. I'll get money off his black ass until one of the other bosses gets tired of him. They'll take care of him one day but we're done. I'm getting a divorce. "

"That's King and Vari's father, Alexus. He's the father of your kids. You know Vari will not live without her brother."

Alexus took another swig of water and gave Rita an incredulous look. A teardrop cascaded down from her left eye and paused for two seconds on the middle of her cheek before continuing down to her chin. "You divorced Papi."

"Not for cheating."

"A lie is a lie," Alexus countered.

For this Rita had no reply. She had divorced Alexus's father — deceased Costilla Cartel boss Juan "Papi" Costilla — when he had come clean about his involvement with the Costilla Cartel, and once he was indicted on federal drug charges and arrested in a raid on their home, she'd taken Alexus and left him for good.

It was ironic that Alexus was now the boss of the Costilla Cartel.

"Your sister left the hospital a week ago," Rita said. "She's back in Chicago and staying with Porsche for now."

Blake's black Maybach was parked in between two white Mercedes vans in the hangar when they made it to LAX and pulled up beside one of the Boeing 767s that Alexus used to transport her vehicles around the world with her while she relaxed in her Gulfstream 650 private jet, usually spending money online in one way or another.

Leaning back on the hood of the gaudy foreign car, Blake wore a black Balmain shirt over matching jeans. Louis Vuitton's "LV" logos decorated his sneakers, belt, and skullcap. Three letters — MBM, which stood for Money Bagz Management, his record label — made up the black diamond-encrusted pendants that hung from his two long gold and white diamond necklaces. There were round-cut white diamonds gleaming in his Hublot watch and bracelet. Larger white diamonds shined on his two pinkie rings. Even his teeth — recently changed from platinum to gold — were blinging with white diamonds. He held a double cup of Lean in his right hand, a fat blunt in the other.

13

Three MBM rap artists — Will Scrill, Young Meach, and Biggs, all dressed just as gaudily and each holding their own cups and blunts — were standing around Blake.

All of them looked at the fleet of Rolls-Royces until the Phantoms parked. Sergio, Enrique's round-bodied nephew, pulled the wheelchair out of the trunk and rolled it around to Alexus's door. Blake set his cups down on the shiny hood of his Maybach and rushed over to help her into the wheelchair.

"Happy Birthday, baby," he said, pecking his lips on the the middle of her forehead as she settled in and gazed at him with frigid eyes.

A wheelchair accessible ramp was resting against the Gulfstream's open door, and standing alongside it were twelve armed men in black suits and sunglasses.

Alexus scowled at Blake. "I fucking hate you, do you know that? And who's the stripper? What's her fucking name?"

Blake grinned and took a step back. "Nobody."

"I don't care who she is. I'm not gonna get her killed. You enjoy yourself. You and that bitch. I'll file for divorce later this week. We can share custody."

She saw the harsh reality of their break-up register on Blake's face. He loved both of his children; losing either of them in a custody battle would emotionally wound him, and Alexus knew it.

He paused for a long moment. By the time he spoke, Rita was out of the Rolls and standing behind the wheelchair.

"We'll talk later," he said finally.

"You'll talk to my lawyers," Alexus countered. "You can run the family business for now, but only until I'm healthy enough to manage things myself. Then I don't ever wanna see you again unless you're picking up the kids. Comprende?"

Blake said nothing.

Stone-faced, he stared after Alexus as Sergio wheeled her to the private jet and up the ramp. She glanced back several times but had no regrets.

Her main focus was getting physically fit again and going back to being the boss of the drug world.

She didn't need Blake to do that.

King Rio

Chapter 2

More than two hundred armed soldiers and high-ranking Costilla Cartel members were standing alongside the private landing strip behind Alexus's megamansion in Matamoros, Mexico when her Gulfstream jet landed.

Alexus paid them no mind. Rita helped her into a waiting Range Rover and two minutes later they were in her ten-car garage.

Wheeling Alexus into the mansion, Rita said, "Don't let what's going on with Blake stress you out. You don't need stress at a time like this. You need to be healing. Let Jesus heal your wounds and your heart. You'll be fine."

Alexus was swallowing more water when her son, King Neal Costilla, came running to her, followed by his nine-year-old big sister Savaria King, Blake's daughter from a previous relationship, and Tamera, their babysitter.

"Mommyyyyyy!" King Neal screamed, smiling from ear to ear. He hugged Alexus gently. "I love you, Ma!"

"I love you, too, Ma," Savaria added. She always called Alexus her mother. Her biological mother had been killed years prior.

Rita pushed the wheelchair to the high-ceilinged family room. The kids walked alongside Alexus, already talking her ear off. King spoke of a fight he'd had with Vari yesterday; Vari claimed it wasn't a fight and it definitely wasn't yesterday. Vari said she and King had been having a lot of fun riding their horses lately; King said yeah, he'd had fun... until he'd fallen off the back of his horse and hurt his arm.

"It was her fault!" he said, pointing an accusatory finger at Tamera, who snickered and replied, "Hey, I told you to hold on."

A 24-karat gold Monopoly board was sitting in the middle of the floor in the family room, its pieces scattered here and there. Alexus shook her head but said not a word. Vari noticed the head shake and immediately went to work putting the board game away.

"King's the one who did it," she muttered.

Alexus looked at King and pointed at the game. "Help your sister clean that up."

He pouted and crossed his arms over his chest.

"Don't make me say it again, King." Alexus gave him the look that said she wasn't messing around.

"Tamera," Rita said, stepping around to the front of the wheelchair, "go and get me a belt. It's about time for King to get some act-right in his life."

Suddenly King was all for putting away the game, especially when Tamera returned with the belt.

Alexus stood up for the first time since leaving the hospital and walked slowly to the sofa. It was an Italian leather sectional that she'd purchased in Ibiza, all white with gold stitching. She sat down and felt a hundred times better. The white sweat suit she had on was loose-fitting and just as comfy. QUEEN was written across the chest of the sweatshirt in large gold letters; it went perfectly with the sofa.

Rita turned on the television — an 80-inch smart TV— and turned to CNN.

Alexus was not surprised to see that the breaking news was all about her. Don Lemon had the story, and he was milking it for all it was worth.

'Alexus Costilla is no longer in a coma, and she's also no longer in federal custody. According to court documents obtained shortly after CNN cameras caught the American billionaire leaving the courthouse in Los Angeles in a wheelchair, Alexus posted a forty-million-dollar bail and is due in court next month on charges of allegedly masterminding a Mexican drug cartel from right here in the US. Federal officials believe she inherited the notoriously violent cartel from her father when he passed away a few years ago after suffering a gunshot to the chest behind a northwest Indiana nightclub.

'The Costilla Cartel is believed to have made tens of billions of dollars smuggling kilos of cocaine and heroin into a number of countries, including the United States, Canada, and even as far away as the UK and Iceland. An informant alleges that Alexus and other higher-ranking members of the cartel were in cahoots with American politicians, judges, and numerous police departments and federal agencies.

'However, there has been a twist in the case. The main informant was found dead with a gunshot wound to the head several weeks ago. His body had been dumped in the Rio Grande. Apparently, he was the main source of information for the entire investigation. There have been no arrests or leads in his murder, but the informant's identity has been revealed, and he's none other than Flako Costilla, Alexus Costilla's uncle.

'Now the question looms: Was Alexus in any way connected to the death of her uncle? Some are saying yes, but there truly is no possible way she could have been involved in Flako Costilla's murder. She was already in a coma when federal agents arrested many of the Costilla Cartel's top echelon members, and he was dead by the time she came out of the coma early this morning...'

Alexus shook her head and rolled her eyes. I don't wanna hear this shit, she thought as Rita took a seat next to her.

"They're, uh, looking forward to you being in charge of things again," Rita said, obviously speaking of the members of Alexus's cartel. "Blake's been being the same old selfish Blake, you know. Your guys aren't feeling it."

"Have you talked to Mercedes?" Alexus drank more water. The ache in her throat was beginning to wane.

"Yeah. Yesterday."

Alexus frowned at her mother's terse reply. "Is something wrong?"

"She said she doesn't want anything more to do with us. Not while you're still in deep in what's going on here in Mexico. That suicide bombing terrified her."

"That bitch."

"Hey. Watch your mouth."

"I lost my husband taking up for her."

"Yeah, well, if you lost him, he didn't want to stay in the first place. Don't waste your time thinking about that mess. Like I told you, God will see you through this and a better man will come. You just focus on getting yourself together. Let go and let God. He's the only one I can guarantee will never let you down."

Alexus gritted her teeth together and pretended to find interest in what Don Lemon was saying.

A minute later Britney Bostic, Alexus's personal attorney, walked in with Dr. Melonie Farr, a psychologist who'd gone from operating an office in downtown Chicago to working full time with Alexus. The two women were Alexus's very best friends, though they strived to keep their relationships based solely on business.

"Britney," Alexus said, "I wanna be divorced from Blake by the end of the week. Also, I'd like you to phone Enrique at your earliest convenience and tell him to brutally murder every bitch Blake has stuck his dick in since I went into that coma."

Chapter 3

Alexus took a bath an hour later, during which time she ruminated over her situation and prayed that the outcome of her trial would not be a lifetime in some federal prison.

She decided she'd go on the run like Assata Shakur before she spent the remainder of her life in prison. She most certainly had the money to disappear. She had over $70 billion in drug money stashed in accounts in the Cayman Islands, another $50 billion stashed all throughout a hilltop mansion in Malibu, California, and a legitimate $72.1 billion net worth that came from Costilla Corp, her entertainment and media corporation that was currently News Corp's number-one rival.

Although the vast majority of Americans would be completely content with such a staggering net worth, Alexus was not. Bill Gates had $79.3 billion. Carlos Slim had a $72.9 billion net worth. Warren Buffet had $72.3 billion.

Alexus was technically number four on the Forbes Magazine list of the world's richest people, and she didn't like it one bit. Sure, she had more money altogether, but she wanted to surpass everyone in net worths as well. She'd been #1 before, and the feeling had been glorious.

She soaked in warm water for twenty-five minutes and then soaped up and rinsed, trying unsuccessfully to keep her mind off her husband's infidelity.

"Fuck you, Blake," she said when she could no longer ignore the ache in her heart. "All the shit I did for your black ass, and this is the fucking thanks I get? I MADE you!"

There was a knock at the bathroom door just as she was getting ready to get out of the tub.

"Lexi, are you in there talking to yourself?" It was Britney. "Mind if I step in? We should talk some things over."

"Come in." Alexus wore an expression of pure anger. She hardly gave the limber young attorney a glance as Britney joined her in the bathroom. "I lost my baby, lost my no-good husband, and maybe even lost my freedom forever, Britney. What the fuck is wrong with my life? Am I cursed? I feel like that guy Job in the Bible, like God's letting Satan drag me to hell and back."

Britney stood next to the tub with her hands on the hips of her creme-colored Prada jumpsuit. She was a slim, dark-skinned goddess with an ever-present smile.

"You're not about to make this a pout fest, Alexus. Be glad that you're alive. Be glad that you survived that blast. Not many women have gone through what you've gone through and come out sane on the other end."

Alexus was grinding her teeth together. Her hands were balled into fists. Her adrenal glands were throbbing.

"Blake and the kids were almost killed a couple of weeks ago. Your mom, too," Britney went on. "The Zetas are rebelling against your cartel. So are the Sinaloas. They wreaked havoc in Los Angeles searching for Blake, literally killing dozens of people."

"I wish they would've got his black ass."

"Don't say that."

"Why not? I mean it. People should always say what they mean and mean what they say. Did you tell Enrique what I said?"

Britney nodded. "Didn't want to, but I did."

"I'm not bullshitting. I want every last one of those bitches dead. Let's see how his dumb ass feels about that."

"You know he has another child, right?"

Alexus's eyes shot to Britney. "Another child?"

"Yes." Britney nodded. "By a girl named Tiffany Jenkins. The kid's name was Timothy Trice, Jr, I'm guessing after the guy she thought was his father at first, but it's now been changed to Blake King, Jr. The kid's the same age as King, stays in Atlanta with his mom. Blake's been bringing him around King and Vari a lot lately."

"That fucker," Alexus muttered in disbelief. "That fucking bastard."

"Calm down, Lexi."

"I should kill him."

"No, you shouldn't. He's your husband."

"Not for long, he isn't."

"Just relax a little. Let him live his life, and you live yours. Trust me, he'll come crawling back when he sees you've moved on. You've gotta focus on recuperating from these injuries and raising your son. That's it. You're a mom, Alexus. Act like it."

Alexus was gritting her teeth again. She wanted to call Blake and give him a piece of her mind. How dare he treat her like this, and while she'd been in a coma, at that. A part of her wanted to order Enrique to kill Blake. It wasn't like he didn't deserve it.

She got out of the tub and dried off. Britney helped her dress (a simple white-lace Victoria's Secret bra and panties set) and take care of her hygiene, then the two of them walked out to the master bedroom.

Alexus got beneath the covers of her king-size bed and immediately picked up the phone from her nightstand. Britney sat at the foot of the bed facing her.

"Who are you calling?" Britney asked, just as Rita and Melonie entered the room.

"Enrique," Alexus said.

Britney sighed.

When Enrique answered, he said, "Come on, now, Alexus. Are you serious?"

"All of them, Enrique. Every single one of them."

"What good would that do? Shouldn't we be all about beating these charges the feds are trying to pin on you?"

"Are you questioning my orders?"

Enrique paused for a brief moment; then: "I'm on it. Our guys are on it. I just sent after Barbie. That's the girl he's been with for the past couple of months."

"Thank you." Alexus slammed the phone down and winced as one of the stitches in her forearm snapped. "Ugh," she growled.

Rita laughed once as she sat down next to Alexus. "Don't lose your mind over that man."

"Let's go over the charges," Britney said as she pulled an iPad from inside her large white shoulder bag. "Most serious charges first. Okay, first off, they've got twenty-nine counts of murder—"

"Twenty-nine!" Alexus was incredulous. "I've never killed that many people."

"They're alleging you ordered the murders. And don't ever say that again. As far as they're concerned, you've never killed anyone at all, not even that Janautica girl you were charged with killing in self-defense that time."

Alexus continued rubbing her arm and listened to the long list of felonies she was charged with. Murders, numerous attempted murders, drug trafficking, kidnappings, criminal confinements— the list went on and on. They were making her out to be a bigger threat to society than Pablo Escobar, which she was, but they weren't supposed to know it.

"I've got something that'll destroy every shred of evidence they have," Rita said. "The security camera footage of those CIA visits, when they were helping you move the drugs into the country from Mexico. We've got the Director of the CIA and the Director of the FBI on tape talking to you. What will they be able to say about that?"

"Hopefully nothing," Britney said. "Hopefully that alone will result in the charges being dismissed before we ever make it to trial. Until then, Alexus, you need to stay out of the spotlight. No more run ins with the law. They'll be looking for a reason to come after you and revoke your bond. You saw the look on that judge's face. It would make his day to have a person of your status sitting in jail."

"Tell her about the Mediterranean cruise," Melonie said.

Alexus frowned. "The Mediterranean cruise?" She looked from Melonie to Britney.

"It is a good idea," Britney said.

"What's a good idea?" Alexus was lost.

"Dr. Farr and I have been planning a getaway. There's a cruise ship that would take us all across the Mediterranean— Italy, Spain, you know. We can visit Vatican City. Who knows, we might even see the Pope. You can come with us. It'll keep you out of all the drama that's been going on here in the States."

Alexus was already shaking her head. "No. No, no, no. I'm not leaving, and neither are you two. Wanna take a boat ride? We've got The Omnipotent. We can take it out for a nice long ride across the Pacific. I've got another yacht in Miami. We can take that one, if you want. But we're not leaving the country. Not as long as Blake's here. I want him to see me every single day until someone kills him."

Rita shook her head. "You are as crazy as your father was, do you know that? You're losing your mind, Lex. Over a man."

"He's more than just any man. He's my husband. I have the right to lose my mind over him," Alexus said.

Suddenly she didn't feel like sitting in bed. She got up and went to her walk-in closet, where she selected a fresh white shirt and shorts set and a pair of white Nike Air Max sneakers.

"What are you up to now, Lex?" Rita shouted from the bedroom.

"It's my twenty-third birthday," Alexus replied. "I'm going out to celebrate it."

King Rio

Chapter 4

Tasia "Baddie Barbie" Olsen's brand-new, hot pink Bentley convertible was the car she'd always dreamed of having.

Her relationship with Blake "Bulletface" King had made her dream a reality.

Riding around the west side of Atlanta with her older sister Fantasia, dressed from head to toe in the finest of Gucci's 2015 summer collection, her pink-dyed hair blowing in the wind as she listened to a K. Michelle song on the radio, Baddie Barbie had no worries.

"I'm so mad they didn't get his ass," Fanny said, shouting to eclipse the loud music.

She was talking about a shooting in Chicago that had not gone as planned. She and Barbie suspected Blake and Alexus Costilla of being involved in their sister Jantasia's disappearance, and they wanted him dead for it. Two days ago they'd set it up so that a gang member in Chicago could kill Blake, not knowing that Blake's own gangsters would be there to shoot back at his attackers, foiling the hit.

"We'll get him." Barbie laughed. "Shit, his dumb ass can't even tell that we're related. He still thinks we're just some freaky hoes from the A. We got time. We just gotta plan it out better, maybe get some niggas here in Atlanta to do it this time."

"Nah, let's get him to Harlem. Beeyo will smoke that nigga for free," Fanny said.

The Olsen sisters were originally from Harlem, though the two of them had been in Atlanta for several years now. Barbie was one of the most sought after strippers in all of Georgia. She had the kind of tight body and meaty derrière that made men drool at the sight of her, and the fact that it was all natural made them want her even more. She'd dated four professional athletes in the past. She'd had a fling with Gucci Mane before he went to prison. Yo Gotti had courted her for a day back when she first moved to Atlanta and started working at Onyx. Men with regular jobs knew that they had absolutely no chance of getting a word out of her, because all her attention was given to the big ballers. If you didn't have a multimillion-dollar net worth, you didn't have a chance with the yellowbone dime piece.

Fantasia, on the other hand, was a successful married woman with a house full of children and a string of luxury car dealerships in three cities. Her husband — a high-ranking Blood out of Kansas City — was now back in federal custody following a drug sting that had spanned eight cities in three states. Fanny still had it going on physically, though she always complained about the bit of gut she had leftover from her pregnancies.

"It's crazy," Barbie said, "we set that nigga up, and he ain't got a clue it was us."

"That's 'cause we fucked the shit out that rich nigga. Blinded his ass." Fanny laughed. "You know, at first I just wanted him dead. For Janny. But now I don't know. I mean, he is a fucking billionaire. The nigga just bought you a Bentley. We might need to keep him around. Maybe these blessings are meant for us. He might be looking out because he feels bad about whatever they did to Janny."

Barbie shrugged her shoulders. "Whatever the case, that nigga can keep right on breaking bread. I'll take every dollar he got for me. Bitches at the club hate my guts now. I'm making more money than I was making dancing, and all I'm doing is sucking Blake's dick every day."

Just then, Barbie's iPhone rang, and Blake's contact picture — him reclined in a seat on his private jet with a pile of cash on the table in front of him — popped up on the screen.

She looked at Fanny and smiled as she answered the call.

"What, boy?"

"Where you at?" he asked.

"In the A, why?"

"I'm on my way back to Chicago. Meet me there."

"I am not about to get on no plane right now, Blake. Me and my girl finna hit up Lenox Square mall and blow some of those bands you gave me."

"I'd listen to me if I were you."

"What's that supposed to mean?"

Blake paused. "Alexus is out of the coma. She's out on bail."

"And...?"

"Ain't no telling what she gon' do to the bitches I been fuckin' with. You might wanna lay low."

Barbie sucked her teeth. "Negro, please. I'm not worried. You enjoy yourself in Chicago. Call me when you get back to Atlanta."

"A'ight. Don't say I didn't warn you. I'm telling you, my wife is crazy for real."

"Yeah, well, I am too. Let the bitch bring it. I'll stomp her ass out in these red bottoms. Hmm. Let her play with it."

"You don't know what you're saying, but okay. I'll be in Atlanta later. Love."

Barbie was all hyped up as the call ended. She turned to her sister and said, "This nigga think I'm supposed to be scared 'cause Alexus is out."

"Scared of what? Ain't that bitch all banged up anyway?" Fanny rolled her eyes and twisted her neck. "That bitch better chill before she fuck around and end up right back in that hospital."

"For real." Barbie high-fived her sister and stepped on the gas. She had $70,000 in cash that she was about to blow at the mall. There was no time to worry about Alexus Costilla.

King Rio

Chapter 5

Blake tried to put all his creative energy into the song he was recording on his iPhone, but the thought of his wife being back in play was far too troubling to ignore.

He'd just landed in Chicago twenty minutes prior and was now sitting in the backseat of his clean black Mercedes Maybach S600 with a double-stacked Styrofoam cup of Lean on ice and a blunt in his right hand. He was high and in a good Codeine-induced daze. Meach, the MBM rapper who was the label's second most popular artist, was next to him with his own cup of Lean and a corpulent blunt of the best Kush in the city.

They were headed to the studio at Blake's Highland Park mansion.

"Alexus gon' act a fool, watch. I know it." Blake couldn't stop shaking his head.

"She said she don't care, bruh. You're stressing over nothing."

"This is the same girl who had Enrique n'em kill seven bitches named Whitney when she thought I had cheated on her with a girl with that name." Blake shook his head again, grabbing the blunt from Meach and taking a deep drag from it. "I saw the anger in her eyes. She gon' go nuts, bruh. On King Neal. I feel it comin'. I tried to warn Barbie but her dumb ass wanna play tough. She gon' fuck around and end up dead and missing like her sister."

Meach shrugged his shoulders dismissively and coughed a couple of times.

Blake also choked on the potent smoke. The weed was almost too strong. He looked out his window at passing motorists as his driver lanced down Roosevelt Road.

He had a new driver, since his previous driver, Remo, was recovering from a gunshot wound to the shoulder in California.

The new driver was Nona, an ex-girlfriend of his who he'd been messing around with lately. Biggs, another MBM rap artist who was now following behind them in a black Ferrari with Will Scrill, was Nona's brother.

The girl in the passenger seat beside Nona was Lakita "Bubbles" Thomas, another of Blake's exes who'd started coming back around since Alexus's hospitalization.

Blake feared for both of their lives.

For a short moment he studied Nona's pretty face in the reflection of the rearview mirror. She was a curvaceous Hip Hop video vixen and an urban magazine model from Detroit. Blake had initially began dating her because she was thick and cute-faced like Alexus, but things had taken a horrific turn when Flako Costilla had tried to shoot her in the head in the living room of the very same mansion that they were all now headed to. The bullet had only grazed the side of her head, far enough away from her skull to prevent certain death but close enough to leave a deep gash in its wake. The shooting went down on the night that T-Walk and Blake had shot each other outside a northern Indiana nightclub, when Blake had misfired his gun and accidentally killed Juan "Papi" Costilla, Alexus's father.

Bubbles had been through her own share of troubles with Blake. Everything from setting up his enemies and becoming involved in several murders to turning into a stripper to keep track of Cup's actions after Blake's daughter was kidnapped, Bubbles had done it all.

Bottom line, Blake had a lot of love for both Nona and Bubbles.

He didn't want anything bad to happen to either of them.

"Don't look so down," Nona said when she noticed Blake's somber expression. "I thought you wanted Alexus out of the hospital. You don't look too happy about it."

"Don't worry about us," Bubbles said, reading his mind. "We'll just stay away from her, okay? Let her keep her crazy ass in California, and we'll stay here in Chicago or at the other house in Miami."

"Or with Tiffany in Atlanta. It's fun there. Her and Danielle are a trip," Nona added with a laugh.

Just then, Blake's iPhone 6 rang.

It was Alexus's mobile phone number.

"Awww shit," Meach said. "That's Queen A right there, ain't it?"

"Shhhh. Everybody be quiet for a minute. Let me talk to this nutcase," Blake said.

Reluctantly, he answered the call and held his breath until Alexus spoke.

"Hey." One word from the richest woman in the world.

"What's up?" Blake passed the blunt back to Meach, suddenly wishing he was sober.

"Oh, nothing. Just missing my hubby, you know. My lovely man."

"Go on somewhere with that crazy shit."

"Did you forget what today is?"

He hadn't forgotten. "Happy birthday."

"That's it? Don't I get a gift or something? You're the richest rapper in the game because of me, and all I get for my twenty-third birthday is a measly 'happy birthday'?"

Blake sighed.

Nona was driving through the parted wrought iron gates at the Highland Park estate. Groundskeepers were tending to the lawn. In the circular driveway, Blake's 45-foot Bulletface tour bus was parked behind two black Rolls-Royces and two black Bugatti Veyrons.

"I bought you something," Blake said. "Just wanted to give you some time to get settled in. You just got out of a coma."

"Okay, so where is my gift?"

"Let me call you back."

"If you hang up on me that bitch you've been fucking will be dead by midnight, you got that?"

Blake lowered the phone from his ear and stared at it for two brief seconds.

Then he pressed end.

He had no idea which of his lovers Alexus had just threatened, and quite frankly he didn't care.

As much as he hated to admit it, he was ready for a divorce from the maniacal drug cartel boss.

She was turning into her father, who'd been the single most terrifying person Blake had ever met, and he no longer wanted anything to do with her.

Her pulling the gun on him before the suicide bombing that had resulted in her hospitalization had been the last straw.

Chapter 6

"He hung up on me!"

Alexus looked around the table at Rita, Britney, and Melonie. The four of them were in the Matamoros megamansion's courtyard, shaded beneath a Mexican flag umbrella and eating a dinner of shrimp, lobster, and crab cakes. Mimosas were their beverages of choice. The sun hung low in the sky, bringing globules of perspiration to Alexus's hairline.

She picked up her cocktail glass and swallowed her drink in one gulp.

No one at the table said a word in response to her complaint of Blake's hanging up on her.

"Enrique!" she shouted.

Enrique and his pot-bellied nephew Sergio were four tables away, watching as Pedro Costilla and a dark-skinned lady friend of his jogged around the outdoor swimming pool with a group of ten Costilla Cartel soldiers in camouflage uniforms.

"Yes, Alexus?" Enrique said.

"Is someone on the way to kill that bi—"

"Si, si." Enrique nodded. "I sent two of our best men. They were already in Georgia. They should be calling me any minute now."

"Dead! I want her dead, Enrique!" Alexus had a blazing fire in her voice.

Rita reached across the table and placed a palm over the back of Alexus's hand. "Let God lead you, Lex. Not the devil."

"That black bastard deserves everything I'm about to have done to that whore."

"She's a woman like you, Alexus —"

"She's nothing like me!"

Alexus got up and stormed off into the mansion. She didn't want to hear her mother's incessant pleas to let Blake's cheap slut live. Blake was lucky that she wasn't sending someone to kill him instead of the girl.

When Alexus looked back over her shoulder, Enrique was five steps behind her.

"Wait." He grabbed ahold of her wrist. "Calm down before you irritate your wounds again. I'm giving an eighteen-year-old Mexican Mafia gangster and his father, who's also La Eme, $50,000 apiece. They're both on their way to pay Tasia Olsen a visit in Atlanta. She has an Instagram account that Mercedes told me about, and on it she just posted a pic with her sister in front of Lenox Square Mall." With a growing smile, Enrique dug in suit jacket's breast pocket and took out a Cuban cigar. "Our guys saw the picture. They know who they're searching for." He put fire from a 24-karat gold Zippo lighter to the end of the cigar and smirked around it as he turned the burning tobacco into a glowing red circle. "Barbie will be dead before sunset. Now go and rest up, enjoy your twenty-third birthday in peace. When they catch up with Barbie, you can watch it on Facetime. Your orders."

Alexus sighed triumphantly. Her face relaxed.

Suddenly she wasn't so upset.

"I love you, Enrique. You haven't let me down yet," she said, and then surprised Enrique by snatching the cigar out of his mouth and planting a juicy kiss on his lips.

Alexus would never be able to explain exactly why she gave Enrique the kiss. She'd always considered him a pretty handsome guy, but she'd looked up to him more than anything.

Now, though, her lips attacked and pulled on his, drawing them into her mouth as she licked and kissed them.

He shoved her away gently. "Stop it, Alexus. I'm your right hand." But he was smiling like a fool. Obviously the feel of her lips had done something special to him.

She gazed at him for a short moment, then thought of how ugly she must look with her wounds and stuffed the cigar back in his mouth.

"Bring me a pound of weed and a lot of blunts. That's all I'm going to do until I'm all healed up— smoke myself back into a coma... before I end up killing every soul Blake knows. Make sure

I get that Facetime video." She went in the bedroom and slammed the door shut in Enrique's face.

King Rio

Chapter 7

"Yo, we need to keep Blake around. For real," Barbie said to Fanny as the two of them sat at a table inside The Cheesecake Factory. "I think I can talk him out of some more bread. Just off that shit he's saying about his wife. I'll tell him to give me enough dough to get away. I bet he'd go for it."

Fanny rammed a forkful of original style cheesecake in her mouth and chewed hungrily.

"Big sis...it is not that serious."

Barbie got two middle fingers and a laugh for the snide remark.

"No, but you're right. He does have a shitload of dough. Let's ask away. Fuck it. I'm with you." She took another big bite of the delicious cheesecake.

Barbie ate from her own plate of the sweet cake.

Two minutes later Fanny added, "I got my gun in my purse. If you see anything funny just reach in there and get it. It's already off safety, so all you'll have to do is start blasting."

Barbie flicked her eyes back and forth from her own purse to her sister. "If you think I'm not strapped, you're a damn fool. Let that bitch send somebody at us if she wants to. I'll send em right back to that hoe in a pine box."

There was another high-five. They finished eating and left the restaurant, headed for the Gucci store.

A young Hispanic man in a dark gray business suit fell in step behind them.

King Rio

Chapter 8

His name was Alejandro Gonzalez, and he'd only been home three weeks.

He'd just spent the last seventeen months of his life in jail for a double homicide that took place in Augusta, Georgia three years ago. The case had gotten thrown out due to lack of evidence after the prosecution's star witness was found murdered in his grandmother's back yard. Although Alejandro had only killed one of the two murder victims (his father, Fernando Gonzalez, had shot the second victim), he hadn't said a word to police investigators regarding his innocence. Fernando had saw to it that the witness did not live to stand trial.

Now that he was home, he wanted to utilize the Mexican Mafia to get rich. Since his father was in good with the Costilla Cartel — the Mexican drug cartel that fed their organization — Alejandro knew that he was in the perfect position to make a fortune. He and his father would make $100,000 altogether if things went as planned today.

That was a great start.

A couple of times he caught the two girls glancing back at him. The younger one was cute and she had an ass like Kim Kardashian. Just about every man she passed stopped to stare. Catcalls came frequently. Alejandro briefly considered snapping a picture of her ass to save in his smartphone but he quickly changed his mind.

It made no sense to photograph the woman he was here to kill.

He kept his distance, kept his eyes on the store windows, kept his thoughts off what was about to take place any minute now. He didn't want to blow his cover. Today he was a handsome gentleman in a sharp Armani suit, traversing the famous mall in search of a new watch to go along with the suit. His father was far ahead of them with a young girl they'd met a mile away from the mall. She was shaped liked the girls Hip Hop videos portrayed as beautiful, a stunning redbone in a sexy black halter and boy shorts, a cute-faced girl named Dria from Baton Rouge, Louisiana.

Occasionally, Alejandro flicked his eyes in his father's direction. Fernando and the girl were window-shopping outside Bloomingdale's.

Turning his attention back to Barbie, Alejandro murmured, "Sweet Jesus. The ass on her."

Barbie's curves made his mouth water. She was an amazingly beautiful young woman, with the flawless face of an angel. Just seeing her side profile through the reflection on store windows was enough to drive him wild with lust. She walked like she knew she was the sexiest woman living.

It was then that Alejandro decided he would rape her if he could, before killing her.

All he needed to do was get her to the parking lot, or maybe even to a bathroom. Then he and his father could Facetime the number they'd been told to call and let whoever was on the other end see the murder take place.

Barbie and the girl Alejandro assumed was Barbie's sister went inside the Gucci store, and Alejandro walked right past without even looking their way.

Chapter 9

Tears of anger dripped steadily from the bottom of Alexus Costilla's chin.

She was smoking what was probably the plumpest blunt she'd ever rolled, sitting up in bed with the lights on, the television off, and the door locked.

Her fingers were trembling. Her body was tense. She couldn't stop looking at the stitches and staples and bruises on her skin. The marijuana was one of the strongest strains she'd ever smoked. She inhaled deeply, coughed a couple of times, and filled her lungs again.

Smoking was the only thing that could soothe her torn emotions.

"How in the hell did I end up without a husband?" she asked herself, thinking out loud. "Now I'm sitting here looking like fucking Frankenstein while he crams his dick all up in some broke, bummy ass bitch who was nothing before she met him, just like he was nothing before I met his punk ass!"

There was a metallic knock at the door, and Alexus instantly knew that it was Enrique; he'd lost his left hand in the suicide blast, and now he had a steel prosthetic hand in its place.

"Can I come in?" He had a key.

"I'm not in the mood to talk right now, Enrique. If it's not the Facetime, I don't wanna hear it."

"Our guys have her in their sights. They're waiting for her to either leave the mall or use a restroom. There's a new development with Blake's companions in Chicago. We've learned of two more women he's currently dating."

"TWO MORE!" Alexus screamed. "Are you fucking kidding me!"

"I wish I was."

"I want those bitches dead, too. Come in."

The doorknob twisted and in walked Enrique. He locked eyes with Alexus immediately.

"Stop crying," he said, and tossed her the iPad he had in his prosthetic hand. "Look. Those are the women. Instagram tells it all." He laughed. "I'll never understand why people put all their business on social media. You don't need to be on there anymore, either. That's how the suicide bomber found you last time."

Alexus only heard the first half of what Enrique was saying.

When she looked at the Instagram page and saw the picture of Blake standing next to his tour bus between two women, Alexus's tears dried up almost instantly. Her distraught expression was replaced by a mask of tension.

"That bitch Bubbles." She spoke through clenched teeth. "And Nona. He's sleeping with them again?"

"Si." Enrique nodded. "There are a few others, I think, but those are the main two. They practically live with him. He's even brought them out onstage at a concert in Philadelphia."

"I want their asses dead, too. Preferably today."

Enrique shut the bedroom door and leaned his back against it. "You might wanna put a little more focus on what Britney has to say. She's a good lawyer. Your mind should be on beating those charges, not ordering hits on innocent people out of jealousy. That's how your sister's mother ended up dead."

"Jealous?" Alexus gave Enrique a cold stare. "Jealous of who? Even now, with my body looking the way it is, I'm still badder than either of those bitches could ever dream to be."

"Never said you weren't."

"I want Blake dead."

"Give the word."

"I should. I really fucking should."

"It's up to you."

"It's all Blake's fault!"

Enrique nodded his head in agreement.

"I'm going to kill Blake, Enrique. I'm telling you now, before it's all said and done, I'm going to cut off his fucking head and hang it up on my wall! How dare he go out and fuck some other bitches while I'm all fucked up in the hospital! And then he has the nerve to have another kid! The same age as our son!"

She flung the iPad clear across the room. It hit the wall next to Enrique's head and dropped to the white fur rug.

Enrique crouched down and picked up the computer tablet just as its screen lit up. He chuckled dryly.

"This is Alejandro calling," he said.

"Alejandro?"

"Yes. One of our guys. He must have the girl in Atlanta."

King Rio

Chapter 10

The second Barbie and her sister walked into the restroom, she grabbed Fanny by the forearm, rushed past two girls that were washing their hands at the sinks, and dipped into a stall.

She dropped her shopping bags on the linoleum floor, dug in her purse, and pulled out her pistol— a .38 Special revolver.

"That Mexican nigga is following us," Barbie said. "I know I'm right. He's been behind us for like twenty minutes. He followed us from The Cheesecake Factory to the Gucci store. He was there again when we left that store. Then he just popped up again when we left the jewelry store."

Fanny put down her own shopping bags and retrieved a semiautomatic pistol from her purse.

They heard the restroom door open.

One of the girls at the sink yelped and said, "This is the lady's room! Excuse you!"

"It's him," Barbie said in an urgent whisper.

"Shit." Fanny pointed her gun at the stall door. "Shit, shit."

Through the narrow crack on the side of the door Barbie saw that it was indeed the Hispanic man who'd trailed them all around the mall. He had an iPhone in one hand, holding it up as if he was recording video.

His other hand was raising a black handgun with a silencer in the barrel.

The same yelp came from the girl at the sink.

The man shushed her.

Then the gun jerked in his hand, and the girl collapsed to the floor with a hand on the hole in her throat.

He shot the second girl in the head. She was dead before she hit the floor.

Barbie gasped and quickly glanced over at her sister.

She and Fanny burst out of the stall and opened fire at the same time.

The man didn't stand a chance. His body rocked from left to right as the rounds tore through his head and chest.

As he fell against the wall, his iPhone slid across the bloody floor and came to rest in front of Barbie's shoe.

There was a woman staring coldly at her through the screen.

When Barbie realized who it was, she put a bullet in the phone.

Chapter 11

Standing at the ceiling-mounted microphone in his studio, with his usual cup of Lean and blunt of Kush in hand, Blake was momentarily at peace. All that mattered was "Pray For You", the song he was recording.

'To be honest, lil daddy, I ain't got a lot to say to you
'Cause you niggas gon' hate soon as I turn my back away from you
So fuck ya kind words, keep gossipin' I'ma spray at you
You should go to church and ask everybody to pray for you

They should really pray for you...
'Cause you hate more than these ladies do
I'm just gettin' bread and hittin' corners in Mercedes coupes
Don't hate on me for that 'cause I earned it, ain't with the lazy group
I been in the studio workin', that's what I'm paid to do
Just to buy my bitch a few Birkins so she can slay for two...
Days before I cop her another, I know you hate it, too
Bought me and my niggas some choppas, don't make us spray at you
Find out where you laying, and lay in the bushes waiting for you
Don't know why you hatin' on me, I never hate on you
If anything I'm making a way for you, get some paper dude
Before I show up in your living room and get to taping you
Up, yup, put that K to you and blow your face in two
Run and we'll be chasing you
Pencil-ass, erasing you
You don't want no rap beef with me, I'll be like Drake to you
Started from the bottom, now I'm on top pullin' caper moves
I got so much cake, that I can feed a fuckin nation, truth
Never been a hater, most you niggas do what haters do
Always hangin wit some lamers that ain't got no game for you

I been at the gun range, sharpening up my aim for you
If you was homeless on the corner, I would have no change for
you
If you somehow came up off hustlin', I would have no caine
for you
How you gonna disrespect the king, I never came for you
Nigga, you the lamest of the lamest of the lamest dudes!
I'll go insane about my change, I'll up and bang at you...'

Blake went on and on for ten minutes and forty-four seconds, his longest freestyle to date. Outside the booth, Bubbles, Nona, and the MBM team were bobbing their heads to the beat and looking at Blake, obviously awestruck by his freestyle.

The iPhones in Blake's pocket were vibrating nonstop. He was glad he'd turned off the ringers before entering the booth, and he hoped the sound of the phone vibrating wouldn't disturb his recording.

When he was done spitting the seemingly endless verse, he exited the booth to a round of applause from his rap artists.

"Nigga," Meach said with the biggest smile, "you gettin' better and better every song, bruh. How in the fuck do you do that shit off the dome like that? You just freestyled some shit most niggas can't even write."

"You're the king for a reason, bruh," Biggs said.

Blake was proud of himself. He had to admit, he'd gone in on that freestyle. As always, he never wrote down anything. The mic and a beat was all he needed to create masterpiece after masterpiece.

He checked his phones to see who'd been calling him like crazy and saw that it was Barbie...and Alexus.

Both of them had called him numerous times in a row. He had eight missed calls from Alexus and five from Barbie.

There were two text messages from Barbie. One read: 'Call me back asap, some shit just went down.' The second said: 'Answer the phone!'

He knew right then that something terrible had happened.

Bubbles saw the look on his face. "You good, bae?" she asked.

He nodded his head yes and excused himself to the hallway, not wanting to interrupt the recording session as Meach settled into the booth.

Nona shadowed him out the glass door. He handed her his Styrofoams as he dialed Barbie's number.

There was no answer.

He tried again, got the same result, and then touched Alexus's number and held his breath until she picked up.

"Almost got that bitch, didn't I?" She cackled. "You know what, Blake? I'm not even mad at you anymore. Honestly. Do whatever you wanna do."

"Alexus —" he started, but Alexus ended the call before he could say more.

He shook his head and looked at Nona.

"What?" Nona's brows rose.

"I think my wife did something to Barbie."

"Something like what?"

"Wish I knew. Barbie ain't answering."

Nona closed her eyes and shook her head, while Blake Googled 'Atlanta news' on his smartphone.

He remembered Barbie saying that she was headed to Lenox Square mall to blow some bands.

The first three news links were all about a shooting at Lenox Square Mall:

'Three dead in Lenox Square Mall shooting. Two suspects being questioned by Atlanta police.'

Blake didn't need to read any more.

He had a feeling Alexus and the Costilla Cartel were somehow involved in the shooting.

"She said, 'I almost got that bitch.' I'm guessing that means she didn't get Barbie. Maybe Barbie got at them before they could get to her." Blake realized that he was really talking to himself.

Nona commented anyway: "You think she'll be coming after me and Bubbles, too? Because if she is, fuck that, I'm going back to Detroit for a while. I'm not about to be on the next First 48."

Blake hugged Nona and rubbed her thick derrière through the small tan shorts she was wearing. Her shirt had a picture of him on the front with Bulletface written across the top and his tour schedule etched across the bottom. The shirt was small enough to expose her diamond belly ring and flat, toned abdomen. The diamond Tiffany's tennis bracelet on her wrist was full of five-carat yellow diamonds and worth $140,000. Blake had gotten it for her last week, and she'd worn it every day since.

She gave him his Styrofoams and he took two tiny sips. He was thinking about Alexus, trying to figure out what he could do to keep his close friends safe while at the same time continuing to live his life without the bothersome constraints of marriage to a cartel boss.

It took him less than five minutes to make up his mind.

"I gotta go and stay with Alexus for at least a few weeks," he said. "To keep y'all safe. She'll have you and Bubbles killed if I don't go and give her crazy ass some attention."

"Do whatever you gotta do, bae. I'm behind you one hundred percent. If that's what it takes to keep her off my trail, then do it. I'm not trying to die no time soon."

Blake chuckled, though he knew the situation was far more serious than either of them could imagine.

He went back in the studio, but only long enough to tell everyone that he had to leave and would be gone for a few weeks.

Then he left for the airport.

Destination: Matamoros, Mexico.

Chapter 12

Three hours had passed since the Lenox Square Mall incident. Alexus had been all smiles ever since.

Although she hadn't succeeded in getting the Atlanta stripper killed, she had made a statement. She wasn't to be fucked with or fucked over. She was the boss and that was that. Anyone who wasn't on board with her would get shoved overboard with no sympathy.

She had the kids sitting up in bed with her. They were watching Shrek 2. King Neal's eyes were glued to the television, but Savaria was more intrigued by her stepmother's ghastly stitches than the animated children's movie.

"Ma, I bet that hurts bad, huh?" Vari asked. She was staring at the stitches in Alexus's left forearm.

Alexus shrugged. "Not really. I'm on pain medications. Vicodin. Makes the pain more bearable."

"What does bearable mean?"

"It means it's not too much for me to deal with."

"Oh." Vari became thoughtful. She put her thumbnails between her teeth and glanced at King. "So, like, when King leaves me alone to watch a movie, it makes him more bearable."

Alexus cracked up laughing. The weed she'd smoked made her laugh even harder. Vari giggled merrily.

"I'm serious, Ma. You know his fat headed self gets on my last nerve every single day. I wish my daddy would've had another girl instead of a boy." Her eyes went wide. "Ooh, have you seen my new brother? His name was Timmy or something dumb like that but now it's Blake like my daddy's. We call him Junior. He looks so much like Fathead over here."

Thinking about Blake's other son made Alexus grind her teeth together in frustration, but she quickly regained her composure.

"No," she told Vari, "I haven't seen him yet."

Vari had gotten her iPhone 6 shortly after Alexus and Blake got theirs, and it hardly ever left her hand. She picked it up from next to her and went to the photo gallery. "Look, that's Junior." She pointed at a picture of a boy standing beside King.

Alexus took possession of the smartphone and zoomed in on the kid's face. Sure enough, he looked like King Neal's twin, and both of them looked exactly like their father.

There was no debating the paternity of either child. They were definitely Blake's children. They had his eyes, his nose, his cocky grin and dark brown complexion.

An emotion that Alexus couldn't quite put a name to swelled her heart with a wonderful feeling. Maybe it was because she was looking at a kid who so closely resembled her only biological child, or because her only child had a brother.

"Makes you feel all weird seeing him and King, don't it?" Vari said. "That's how it makes me feel. I've had another brother for four whole years and I didn't even know it."

"Neither did I." Alexus gave Vari the phone back. "I should hurt your father."

Vari giggled and set the smartphone down behind her. "He had Junior with a different girl. You ain't so happy about that, huh?"

"How'd you guess?"

Vari shrugged. "I just know. I can tell by the look on your face."

"You don't know the half of it."

"I know that my daddy had a new girlfriend when you was in the hospital."

"Don't remind me."

"I think my daddy's stupid sometimes. Not all the time, but sometimes."

"I think you're right about that."

"I wouldn't say it to his face, though."

"Yeah?" Alexus was amused. "Why not?"

"Because he'd probably kick my butt."

"If he kicks your butt I'd kick his."

"You can't kick my daddy's butt." Vari laughed and shook her head. "He's a man, Ma. A woman can't kick a man's butt. Well, maybe some women can. Like those girls that fight in the ring. Laila Ali. She might be able to kick my daddy's butt."

"You're underestimating your Ma. I can kick some serious butt, Vari. My dad taught me how to fight when I was your age. I can handle my own with just about anyone."

Vari laughed again, obviously not believing that Alexus could fight. King literally ignored the two of them until Shrek 2 came to an end.

By then, Alexus and Vari were discussing boys.

There was a white boy in Vari's class who'd asked her to be his girlfriend. Alexus thought it was the absolute cutest thing. She remembered back when she'd experienced the same kind of puppy love in elementary school in Brownsville, Texas. Her childhood boyfriend had ended up being framed for a heinous murder and sentenced to the death penalty years later, when he and Alexus had been in high school.

The actual killer had been Alexus's father, Juan "Papi" Costilla.

"His name is Johnny," Vari was saying. "He wrote me a note asking me to be his girlfriend. I haven't responded yet because I don't like white boys. But he's cute."

It was Alexus's turn to giggle. "Girl, what do you know about cute?"

"I know enough."

"Why don't you like white boys?"

"Because... what if his momma and daddy is racist or something, you know what I mean? What if they hate black girls, like in the movies? I don't wanna be with somebody whose family won't accept me for who I am."

"First of all, you don't need a boyfriend. You're nine years old. All you need is an education and good home-training."

"So, I can't have a boyfriend?"

"Ask your father. If he says yes, then yes."

"No, no... that's not gonna work." Vari looked serious, but it was comical to Alexus, who let out a laugh at the response.

"Why won't it work?" Alexus asked.

"Because my daddy slapped me on my butt harder than a mug last time I mentioned a boyfriend to him. He said he was gonna beat my boyfriend up! Can you believe that? A grown man, wanna hit a child." She shook her head in disbelief. "You know what? Never mind. I'll wait for college. Got too much more math to learn. Ain't got time to be thinking about no boy."

"You're a smart girl," Alexus murmured.

"I know that," Vari said arrogantly. "I mean, after all, I am Alexus Costilla and Blake King's daughter. I have the best ma and the best daddy in the world."

Vari's kind words warmed Alexus's heart, so much so that she lightweight regretted sending the goons after Barbie.

Though she hated the fact that the killers had failed.

"I love you, little lady," Alexus said, and pulled Vari in for a hug. She truly did love Savaria just as much as she loved her son, who was now meddling with Vari's smartphone while she had her back to him.

"Can my new brother move in with us?" Vari asked.

This sparked King's interest.

He got so excited, in fact, that he tossed the phone aside and said, "Yeah, Ma, can he? Please?"

Vari's phone went crashing to the floor.

She turned and scowled at the phone, then at King.

He had the guiltiest look on his face.

"Sorry, sister," he said in a very low tone.

Vari picked up the phone and showed Alexus the cracked screen.

"Now do you see why I wanted a sister? Can't we sell him or something?" Vari's attitude was palpable. "We should sell King for a new iPhone. Sell him to some people in China somewhere, and no refunds."

"You can't sell me!" King said, suddenly irate.

"I'll get you another phone tomorrow, Vari. Relax. We're not selling your brother." Alexus wore the biggest smile.

Savaria's smile was upside down. "Well," she went on, "we should. It's a good idea. An iPhone is a lot more useful than a dingbat."

King's brows furrowed. He turned to Alexus. "Ma, what's a dingbat?"

Before Alexus could answer him, Enrique's metallic knock rattled the bedroom door, and what he said made Alexus's eyes widen in surprise.

"Alexus, your, uhhh... your husband is here. He's coming in now. Should we let him in or what?"

Alexus didn't hesitate.

"Yes, yes. Let him in. I'll be out in a second."

She was out of the bed and in her walk-in closet seconds later. She couldn't let Blake see her in anything but her very best.

King Rio

Chapter 13

"It's way too muhfuckin hot for this Mexico shit," Blake muttered discontentedly as he stopped in the huge mansion's foyer to take a refreshing gulp of iced Lean.

There were armed men in black suits and sunglasses posted along the walls and at the front door, the same kind of men he'd encountered as he'd driven his 2016 Bugatti Veyron Grand Sport up the long, tree-and-flower-lined driveway to the estate's front gate.

They knew Blake — he'd visited the Matamoros mansion numerous times and had even lived here on occasion — but today he didn't trusty either of them. He had no idea how Alexus was feeling. He didn't know if she'd be happy to see him or happy to have him murdered for dating other women.

The stress of being married to a cartel boss was a lot to deal with, certainly more than the average man could handle.

Which is why Blake had hidden his 9-millimeter Glock and two 50-round drums in the stash compartment underneath the driver's seat of his Bugatti before having it loaded onto a cargo plane that arrived at General Servando Canales airport in Matamoros forty minutes after his private Gulfstream jet landed.

Now the gun was in the Louis Vuitton duffle bag he was carrying. He had it unzipped, so that he could easily reach in and grab ahold of the perilous pistol at a second's notice.

He let his guards down a little when King Neal and Savaria came running down the spiral staircase and into his arms. He put down the duffle and his Styrofoam cups and lifted them both up onto his hips.

"Daddy, Mommy's home!" King said.

"He broke my phone, Daddy," Vari said.

"I said sorry!" King fired back.

Blake chuckled and set them down. "Where's Momma?"

"In her bedroom closet." Vari pointed up the stairs. "She said give her a minute."

Enrique appeared at the top of the staircase. He had a cigar in his mouth, and the way he was peering down at Blake was unsettling.

"You here to stay?" Enrique asked.

Blake frowned. "Don't worry about it, nigga. Why you all in my b'ness?"

A crooked smile burgeoned on Enrique's face. He raised his hands, as if in surrender. "Hey, I'm not the one you've gotta be worried about. The queen is out of the hospital, it's her twenty-third birthday, and she's not happy. That seems like your problem, not me. I'm with you until Alexus says otherwise."

Blake glowered at Enrique a moment longer.

Then his attention shifted to Britney Bostic and Rita as they came heading up the hall toward him.

He hugged them both, and Rita led them all to the family room.

Blake felt like he'd just walked onto the set of a Real Housewives taping.

Pedro Costilla and his new girlfriend Mary were sitting on the sofa watching the movie Selma on the massive ninety-inch television. There were glasses of red wine on the glass-top coffee table. Pedro had on a sharp, expensive blue suit, and Mary — like Britney and Rita — wore a ton of diamond jewelry, a tight-fitting dress, and Louboutin heels.

It was like Blake was watching Lifestyles of the rich and famous.

He, on the other hand, was thugged out as usual in all black with two thick gold chains to go along with his gold Rolex watch and the gold spikes on his black Louboutin sneakers.

He sat down in an easy chair and sighed.

King and Vari stood at his knees, the two of them smiling from ear to ear.

He noticed that Rita was giving him the side-eye, and he knew why. Days earlier, during a two-day getaway on Alexus's yacht, Rita had walked in on him getting head from Barbie. He hadn't known until Barbie told him the following morning.

When everyone was seated, Britney asked if he was hungry. He wasn't. He'd eaten a 32-ounce steak, two baked potatoes, and a large serving of mac and cheese on the jet.

"All that Lean is putting a stomach on you," Britney said.

Blake chuckled and went back to talking to King and Vari. He missed them more than they knew. Every time he left them here in Mexico with Alexus, or in California with Rita, his heart grew heavy with guilt.

"Vari got a white boy that wants to be her boyfriend," King said out of the blue.

Vari's mouth dropped open. She reached across Blake's legs and gave King a quick slap to the back of the head.

The blow didn't seem to bother King at all. In fact, his beaming smile grew wider.

"A boyfriend?" Blake said.

Vari put her head down. "He's not my boyfriend, Daddy. He wrote me a note. That's it."

"Don't get that lil boy hurt. I'll go to his house and break his daddy's whole face for even making a nigga that grew up and wrote my baby."

"It's not that serious, Daddy."

"It is to me." Blake's stern voice said it all; he was dead serious.

Britney said, "I don't care what you do while you're here, just don't leave my girl with a broken heart. She's going through enough pain as it is. You should be a source of joy and happiness for her. Here lately you haven't been the best husband—"

"I'm not tryna hear none of that," Blake said, and Britney shut right up.

Pedro was next to speak. "Hope you've got your missile on you. I'm in no mood to be Superman this week."

Over the past several weeks, Pedro had saved Blake's life time after time as the enemies of the Costilla Cartel came for his life. Pedro had shot up a car full of gunmen in Chicago when they were firing shots at Blake as he left out the rear exit of a nightclub. Then he came to the rescue again when some Bloods in Los Angeles had started shooting at the Bulletface tour bus following a Staples Center concert, and finally he'd helped save the entire MBM team from certain death when a squad of rival cartel members came for Blake's head later the same night.

The thought of those rivals coming after Alexus while she was in bad shape gave Blake yet another reason to stay here for a while.

Pedro's girlfriend said hi. He could tell by the way her eyes were stuck on him that she was a fan.

"Daddy," Vari said, "When can we see our new brother again?"

"I'll send for him in the morning." Blake put his Styrofoam cups on the table and settled into the big leather chair. It was white like everything else in the place. White was Alexus's signature color. Blake couldn't remember the last time he ever saw her wearing anything other than white.

Which is why he was shocked when she came walking into the room wearing a long red gown with sleeves that went to her wrists.

She had on red lipstick. A necklace made of red diamonds shined on her neck, and she wore a matching bracelet.

"Yes, girl," Britney cheered, "slay, slay, slay!"

"Look at my baby." Rita was all smiles.

Vari said, "Mommy, you look so beautiful."

Alexus was blushing as Blake stood and walked to her.

If not for her recent injuries, Blake knew that he would have carried her straight to the master bedroom and had his way with her. She was so perfectly built and stunningly beautiful that he didn't know what to do or say. Now the reason for him marrying her was perfectly clear. She was badder than any of the women he'd been sleeping around with lately. She was much prettier, her ass was so much fatter, and her loyalty to him was unparalleled.

He draped his arms around her waist and gave her a long, loving, meaningful hug. He pressed his lips to her cheek and left them there for so long that there were tears in her eyes when she drew back.

"Red?" he said.

Alexus smirked and nodded and thumbed away her tears. "Had to do something to make you look at me again. This time I'm not playing, Blake. If you keep fucking over me this red will be the blood of your little girlfriends whenever we catch them."

"Damn." Blake chuckled at the threat. "I see you ain't changed."

"Nope, not a bit."

"Wanna go somewhere for your birthday?"

"I'm not dressed like this for nothing," Alexus said.

Blake realized then just how much he'd missed his beautiful wife.

King Rio

Chapter 14

The Atlanta Police Department have a mini precinct in Lenox Square Mall, which explained their swift arrival at the restroom after the shooting.

Barbie and Fanny were taken in for questioning, and Barbie ended up charged for the gun but not for the the man's murder. The only reason she caught the gun charge was because she was a convicted felon, but the police assured her that it would more than likely be dropped to a misdemeanor since she and her sister had taken down the man who'd murdered two innocent women in the restroom, a killer with alleged ties to the Mexican Mafia. Fanny's gun was taken for evidence. The murder of Alejandro Gonzalez was tagged as self-defense. After two long hours of giving statements, Barbie paid the $5,000 cash bond for her gun charge, and she and Fanny left the mall in the Bentley, cruising between two police cars that would escort them home.

Fanny was a nervous wreck. She didn't want to talk, and when Barbie turned on the radio, she quickly shut if off.

"I called Blake when they were taking us in," Barbie said. "His ass didn't answer. I'll turn on my phone and call again when we get home. Battery's dead now."

When Fanny didn't reply, Barbie continued. "Now I'm wondering if it was Alexus who did something to Janny. I saw the bitch on that phone, sis. I'm telling you, it was Alexus. She was sitting in bed, just staring at me. The bitch looked evil as fuck. She sent that man to kill us, Fanny. What kind of crazy shit is that?"

Fantasia buried her face in the palms of her hands and shook her head despondently. She couldn't believe what had happened in that restroom. She'd actually killed a man. The vivid memory of the dead women on the restroom floor bothered her even more.

"What the fuck, Barb?" Fantasia said finally.

"I know, big sis. I'm telling you, it's no coincidence that Janny went missing in Mexico when she was with the same crazy bitch who just sent a man to kill us just because I'm fucking Blake. And the more I think about how that nigga threw me into that bathroom mirror at his mansion in Chicago, the more I think his ass might have been the one who did something to Janny in the first place." She slapped her hands on the steering wheel. Her nostrils flared. "I should've never even started fucking that nigga. Fuck his money. I was supposed to smoke his punk ass for Janny. If I would've listened to you we wouldn't be going through this shit now."

Suddenly, Fantasia started crying. "That man killed those women. Alexus sent that man to kill us! That's what we should have told the police!"

Barbie reached over and massaged her sister's shoulder. "Don't trip, sis. I'm gon' take care of this. No more fucking and sucking that nigga for his money. The next time he comes through to see me, I'm calling Beeyo. I'll pay cous' ten G's to wet that fuck-nigga up. Fuck it."

Her eyes flicked in every direction as she drove. Her house was not far from Lenox Square Mall. It was a nice two-story red-brick home on Shadowlawn Avenue, an affluent area in Buckhead where only the well-off resided. Blake had given her $100,000 cash to avoid legal troubles after he'd thrown her into the mirror, and she'd put it all down on the quarter-million-dollar home.

As she was pulling into the driveway behind Fanny's parked Mercedes, the two police cars came to a stop in front of the house.

"You think the Mexican Mafia will be after me now?" Barbie asked Fanny.

"I don't know. I hope not. Maybe you should come and stay with me for a few days. It may not be safe here."

Barbie's fingers tightened around the steering wheel. She shut her eyes and sighed. "Jesus," she said, "please watch over me and my —"

A screeching of tires put her prayer on hold.

Chapter 15

Fernando's face was streaked with tears as he came speeding around the corner onto Shadowlawn Avenue in his green Ford pickup.

He'd followed the police cars here from the mall, and now he was ready. Ready to avenge his son's murder. Ready to take out the no-good whores who'd gunned Alejandro down.

The AK-47 on his passenger seat was all he needed to even the score.

Two seconds later he rammed into the rear of one of the cop cars, sending it crashing into the second one. Fernando's airbag deployed and busted his nose, but he wasn't hurt much.

He unbuckled his seatbelt, pushed open his door, and stepped out with the assault rifle in hand.

Raising it, he approached one of the police cars and shot the two dazed officers dead, then turned and sent a spray of bullets at the two women who were rushing out of the Bentley in the driveway.

"You kill my fucking son! You kill my boy!" He squeezed the trigger again.

The heavier of the two girls screamed and went down as a mist of blood flew out of her.

The second police car's doors swung open. The policemen rushed out with their guns drawn.

Fernando fired at them while walking sideways up the driveway. He heard the girls screaming. He caught a bullet to his left thigh and slapped a hand down over the wound as he turned to finish off the girls.

The girl he'd been paid to kill was dragging the girl he'd shot around the front end of the Bentley.

He took aim at them...just as one of the policemen was taking aim at him.

He felt the stinging rounds hitting his back as he went down. He saw the girl he'd been paid to kill staring at him with fearful eyes. He tried to lift the AK-47 to shoot her but he couldn't lift it, so he just pulled the trigger until the policeman put some more hot lead in him.

These rounds were fatal.

Chapter 16

Blake paid $40,000 to rent out the Oakland-Alameda County Coliseum and another $32,000 to have the staff from West Hollywood's Madeo restaurant prepare a table and food for two in the middle of the field.

An additional $150,000 went to Keyshia Cole for her to sing before and during the scrumptious Italian dinner. $20,000 paid for the four thousand long-stemmed red roses that were situated near the table and the other four thousand that would be delivered to the mansion while they were out celebrating.

Blake's assistant, Kendall Ashland, had handled it all while they were on the jet.

Now, as Blake drove his Bugatti into the stadium where the Oakland Raiders played, Alexus was sitting next to him wearing a blindfold and an unforgettable smile.

"This better be good," she said, squeezing his hand excitedly. "You're not out of the dog house just yet."

"Damn, I'm in the dog house?" Blake laughed. "What kinda shit is that. I'm here for you on your day, surprising you and shit, and I'm still in the dog house?"

"As long as I'm not with you, and as long as you still got a whole fucking team of sluts, your ass is indefinitely in the dog house. Comprende?"

Blake had no response. He didn't need one. He knew that once he removed the blindfold, his actions would speak for him.

He pulled up alongside the table and parked.

"Ready?" He leaned over to Alexus and pecked his lips on her cheek.

She nodded.

He removed the blindfold, and she let out an awestruck gasp.

"Blake!" Her beautiful green eyes went wide, and her hands rose to cover her open mouth.

"Happy birthday, baby," he said as he climbed out of the car and walked around it to open her door.

She was still in shock as he led her to the table. Keyshia Cole began singing happy birthday to her. They stood together and listened.

"This is absolutely amazing, Blake. Thank you so much." Alexus picked up one of the roses and held it to her chest as she swayed side to side to the heartwarming music.

Minutes later they sat down to eat, and Blake pulled a folded sheet of paper from the pocket of his baggy jeans.

"Most men would wear a suit for something like this," Alexus said.

"I'm not most men." Blake unfolded the paper. "I wrote a song for you on the flight here. Well, a verse. For your birthday."

"Awww." She clasped her hands together, beaming. "You know how much I love your music."

"Shut up and listen."

"Fuck you."

He grinned, reminiscing about all the times she'd cussed him out over the years. Then he began the rap verse he'd written for her:

'I love you... that's all I know
Though I'm a street nigga and my heart is cold as the snow
But it gets warm for you...
I never meant to cause no harm to you
I'll never forget all the painful nights you helped me through
When I was shot up you was there
Blessed me with some bands, I swear
Bailed me out the county jail
And had a Chevy waiting there
Half a million in the suitcase
That was all off trappin too
Warned me right before them pussy niggas came and clapped me too
Love you, Lexus, that's the truth
Had my son and that's the proof
Remember when they shot at us in the Chi you was clappin too

Happy birthday, baby girl
To Blake King you mean the world
I'll forever be here for you, always you my crazy girl
You my wifey, got me icy, no more Nikes
Just red bottoms on my sneakers
And my songs from the speakers
I'm strong but every time we kiss I get a little weaker
I love your ass forever...it's fat and always fleeker
Than the rest...I'm the king and you the queen
Just ask the people they'll say yes
Love the way that ass sit up when you step out wearing a dress
I be like Jesus, Yeezus, yes
I'm sorry for all the stress
Just ask me to come and you know my answer will be a yes'

There were tears in Alexus's soft green eyes as he completed the special birthday song and slid the paper across the table to her.

Out of the corner of his eye, he saw a white Rolls-Royce limousine and a white Mercedes Sprinter van driving into the stadium, and he immediately knew that it was Enrique and other members of the cartel.

He paid them no mind.

The look on Alexus's face had his full attention.

"I love you so much, Blake. Thank you. Thank you for all of this. I couldn't have wished for a better birthday."

She leaned across the table and molded her lips against his.

He put his hands on her head and held her face to his, enjoying the succulent feel of her kiss. He never wanted it to end.

When she pulled back, she gazed into his eyes for a long while. Keyshia Cole got to singing again, making the moment even more magical.

He thumbed her tears away. "I love you for real, Alexus. I wanna make this shit work again. We got to. For King and Vari."

"And Junior, huh?" She smiled.

Blake was caught, but it wasn't really a revelation that he'd planned on hiding from her.

"Yeah, I got another young king. I fucked her when you was with T-Walk. Didn't know I'd gotten her pregnant until just recently."

Alexus studied him. Her fingernails drummed on the table as their food was delivered. She looked at her plate of spaghetti and meatballs, her favorite Italian dish, and her smile grew. It was served with a glass of red wine.

"How'd you get this stadium for the night?" She twirled long spaghetti noodles around her fork and slipped it in her mouth.

"My assistant did it."

"You've got a great assistant." Alexus's eyes became stringent slits. "What's the bitch's name? I know you're fucking her."

"No, I'm not. She's married."

"Oh, please. Like you wouldn't fuck a married woman."

"If it was you, I would."

Alexus rolled her eyes and kept eating.

For a few minutes they ate in silence. The smile on Alexus's pretty face made Blake's day. He couldn't stop staring at her. She was his wife, a dime piece Black and Mexican girl with a net worth like Warren Buffet's and an ass like Kim Kardashian's. He was proud to say that he was her husband, even though they were technically separated.

He thought back to the day the two of them had first met. He'd been standing outside in Michigan City, Indiana with a few of his guys, selling crack to the local dope fiends. At the time he'd had just a few thousand dollars and an ounce of crack to his name.

The memory made him feel so good that he had to bring it up to Alexus.

"Remember the day we met?" he said.

"Yeah, you were fat and short...and loyal. I didn't have to worry about you fucking a thousand different bitches. I fucked up when I gave your ass all that money. That's what started all this shit."

Blake didn't want to hear about his cheating episodes.

"Okay, let's talk about something else." He chuckled.

"You're the one who brought the shit up."

"I said the day we met. If I recall, I didn't even get no pussy that day. I got robbed by your cousin, had to go and lay some niggas down about it when I was supposed to be with you."

Alexus snickered with a rope of spaghetti dangling from her lip. "What I do remember is when you showed up at my back door the next morning eating a bag of chips—"

"Doritos," Blake interrupted.

"Yeah. And you pushed past me, went to my refrigerator, took out my carton of orange juice, and drank it all right in my face."

He nodded his head. "Then you threatened to shoot me, and I slid my strap across the kitchen table to you and told you to do it."

"Which I should have done," Alexus said with a voice full of attitude. "Maybe if I'd have put you on a shitbag back then these bitches wouldn't be so quick to fuck you."

Blake couldn't pull away from the memories. "You took me upstairs and gave me that juicy, though." He grinned.

"Biggest mistake of my life." She was grinning, too. "Okay, enough about our history. Let's talk about the here and now."

"Okay. Talk."

A different kind of smile crossed Alexus's face. It was one of those smiles that didn't mean well.

"You talked to your girlfriend in Atlanta today?"

"I knew it. That mall shooting. That was you, wasn't it?"

The treacherous smiled widened. "It's not good to cheat on your wife," she said.

"Is she dead?"

"No. Believe it or not, she actually killed the guy we sent to kill her. Feisty little bitch."

"You ain't gotta do that shit. Leave her alone. I'm done fuckin' with her. I'm all about you from now on."

"I know that you've been fucking those other two bitches again, too. Nona and Lakita. I should have their heads cut off."

"You are evil, you know that?"

"If my father was still around it would be a lot worse."

"You don't think I know that?"

"I know you know. But I don't think you understand just how much I've taken after him."

"Oh, I know."

"You think you know. You really have no idea." She pushed her plate aside and took a drink of wine. "I'll call off the dogs if you promise to stay here with me at least until my trial starts."

"I got shows to do."

She shrugged. "So what? Cancel them. I'll pay you twice as much as you'd make doing those stupid concerts."

"It's not that easy."

"It actually is that easy. You're the CEO. Make a boss call and leave it at that."

She waved over a member of Keyshia Cole's entourage and whispered in his ear. He walked back to Cole and whispered to her.

"The fuck is that about?" he asked.

"A special request."

"What kinda request?"

Seconds later be got his answer.

Keyshia Cole started singing "I Should've Cheated."

"This is dedicated to you," Alexus said, wearing that same diabolical smile that never failed to make him feel uneasy.

He flipped her a middle finger and laughed. "You should've cheated and got a nigga killed for nothin'?"

"Oh, please. As many times as you've cheated on me. I deserve some dick from a new nigga."

"And that new nigga deserves a closed-casket funeral."

They both laughed at that.

Thirty more minutes passed before they got up to leave. Alexus wanted to take her roses home with her, but Blake assured her that she'd have more than enough roses when they got home.

Blake enjoyed watching Alexus walk to the car. He'd almost forgotten how amazing her derrière looked from the back. He couldn't think of a single woman with a nicer backside. Not even Serena Williams could compare to the perfect thickness of it. She was the kind of woman all the rappers wanted.

And she was all his.

When she was seated in the Bugatti, Blake went to the trunk and took out a large white paper bag with the words Le Vian sketched across the side of it in red cursive letters.

Getting in the driver's seat, he handed her the bag "Happy birthday again, baby."

She opened the bag, reached in, and took out the twelve white jewelry boxes that had been stacked up along the bottom of the bag.

Each jewelry box varied in size. Blake's assistant had stopped by the jewelry designer's store with orders to buy every expensive piece of diamond jewelry on display. It ended up costing him $3.2 million.

The glow in Alexus's eyes as she opened the boxes made it worth every dollar spent.

King Rio

Chapter 17

"Thanks a lot for all the peaceful days we've been having. I was getting pretty tired of seeing people die," Mary said to Pedro.

They were in Alexus's Rolls-Royce Phantom limousine with Enrique, leaving the stadium behind Blake and Alexus.

Pedro laughed and toked on his cigar. His mind was on the exact kind of bloodshed that Mary was speaking against.

He couldn't change his thoughts even if he wanted to.

Enrique had just learned the whereabouts of Gamuza, boss of the Los Zetas Cartel and the FBI's most wanted man.

Pedro wanted Gamuza's head. The cartel boss had not only reneged on his promise to merge his cartel under the Costilla Cartel umbrella, but he'd also beheaded Pedro's grandfather a long time ago. The Costilla family had wanted Gamuza dead ever since.

There was only one time that Pedro had seen the powerful old man. It had been at a ramshackle bar in Juarez, when the bosses of all of Mexico's most dominant drug cartels had come together for a meeting on the specifications of their cartel joining the Costilla Cartel. It was made clear then that Alexus Costilla would be the top boss; now, however, neither of them were honoring their parts of the deal.

"I'll do my best to keep the peace," Pedro said, and patted Mary on the knee.

She said, "Do you know that I have yet to tell my parents that I've dropped out of college? They think I'm still in El Paso. My mom keeps asking why she can't come and see me on the weekends like she used to. When she asks where I've been getting all the money I've been sending her, I tell her I've found myself a sugar daddy."

"That's not exactly a lie."

"There a big difference between a sugar daddy and what you are."

"Not really. I'm taking care of you, aren't I? Okay then. I'm your sugar daddy. You weren't lying."

Mary smiled and shook her head at the ridiculous comparison. She and Pedro had yet to make it official. They'd slept in the same bed together twice but not once had he even attempted to have sex with her. The day after her college roommate's funeral they'd flown around the Mediterranean, from Spain to Italy and back to Spain again, sightseeing for the most part and getting to know each other better. Upon their return to the States, he'd contacted her bank and paid off the mortgage on the new home she'd recently moved into in El Paso, Texas, and since then he'd given her over $1 million in drug money. She'd split the majority of the money between four different bank accounts, though every two days or so she spent a few thousand on shopping sprees and wired a few more grand to her family in Indianapolis.

Pedro enjoyed the young woman's company. She was the kind of dark-skinned Black woman he'd always dreamt of being with, the kind that was honest and compassionate, hardworking and loving, all the good characteristics he wanted in a woman. Her stern demeanor kept him doubling over in laughter whenever he was the source of her attitudes. He hoped that soon they would take the next step in their relationship, but until then he was content with just having her around.

"That was so romantic," she said thoughtfully, "what Blake just did for Alexus. And here I was thinking they'd never get back together again."

Enrique chimed in. "Alexus and Blake are like yin and yang, you know? Complete opposites but they can't live without one another. They're always breaking up and getting back together, cheating on each other and all that mess. It's what they do. But I don't think there will ever be a day when they'll leave each other alone."

"I hope not," Mary said. "Black people are just as obsessed with them as we are with Jay and Bey, if not more. No, I take that back — definitely more. Nobody can compare to those two. And they're both real live gangsters. It's like the 2015 Bonnie and Clyde. When I told my girls back home that I've been hanging around Bulletface, they swore up and down I was lying. I had to post the pics I took with him backstage at that Staples Center concert on Instagram for anyone to believe me. The first thing everybody wanted to know was if he was cheating on Alexus like the media claimed he was. Of course I didn't even reply to those questions. I know when to keep my mouth closed."

Pedro scoffed. "I can't tell."

Mary slapped him hard across the chest for the wise crack, and he burst out laughing.

Sergio, Enrique's plus-sized nephew, was in the driver's seat, propelling the extra-long Phantom down Nimitz Freeway. He had the partition down so he could get in on the conversation if the urge struck him, but for now he was just driving and listening.

Suddenly, Enrique began unbuttoning his suit jacket.

"Oh, God," Mary said, and buried her face against Pedro's arm.

She knew that Enrique was about to check on the bullet wound in his abdomen again. He'd been doing it all night.

"For Christ's sake," Pedro said, "leave it alone. You're starting to gross my lady out."

"Starting to?" Mary said sarcastically.

Enrique's deep chuckle ensued. He gave zero fucks. This was the fourth time today he'd checked the wound in front of them. He'd gotten it from Rita Mae Bishop, who accidentally shot him as she was shooting a masked Zeta Cartel gunman who had come to her home to kill her and Blake's children. The gunman was just getting ready to blow Enrique's brains out when she'd opened her bedroom door and opened fire, killing the gunman but also wounding Enrique.

"Doesn't look all that bad, does it?" Enrique asked Pedro.

"You're fine. Shit, Enrique, if you keep unbandaging that wound it's gonna look a lot worse than it does now."

"I thought that fucker standing in front of me would have had bigger balls, seeing that he was a Zeta and all. He did all that shooting and then stopped to talk to me." Enrique laughed. "Last I checked, threats have never killed anyone"

"Bottom line, he was with the wrong cartel. That's all there is to it." Pedro glanced over at Mary, and when he spoke again it was in Spanish instead of English. "So, what are we going to do about Gamuza? We know where he is— now what?"

Enrique also spoke in Spanish. "Alexus has to do it." His tone was a lot more serious than it had been a couple of seconds ago. "There's nothing that can solidify her grip on Mexico more than if she becomes known as the one who killed that old devil. El Chapo might even back off a little. You never know."

"I'll tell you what I do know," Pedro said. "It needs to happen immediately. Not next month, not next week, but as soon as humanly possible. There's no telling how long he'll stick around at that location. We have to get him now."

Mary cleared her throat. "Umm, excuse me. Y'all don't see me sitting here?" She waved a hand in the air. "It's rude to just talk in an alien language in front of company." She turned to Pedro. "And if you're talking about some more drama, count me out. I'm going back to my house. Y'all can go and shoot up whoever, but I won't be here to see it."

During the few weeks she'd known Pedro, Mary had witnessed over twenty murders, including the murder of her dear friend Lisa.

She didn't want to see any more bloodshed.

Little did she know, a fair amount of bloodshed was in her immediate future.

Chapter 18

There was something about a woman in red that drove Blake wild.

He was focused so unwaveringly on the generous humps her ass made in the gown that he nearly tripped over his own feet following her through the door when they made it back to the Matamoros mansion.

No matter how many times he visited the massive home, it always had a way of leaving him spellbound every time he returned. The heated white marble floors, the expensive, gold-framed paintings and vases that lined the walls, the high ceilings and the dozens of butlers and maids and chefs that tended to the family's many needs — it was all more than he could have ever imagined as a kid in little old Michigan City, Indiana.

Tonight was the first time the mansion's elaborate décor didn't grab his attention.

Alexus had him hypnotized.

She looked back at him and smiled as they entered the foyer.

It was filled from wall to wall with red roses.

"You're really putting it on heavy today, aren't you?" Alexus said. "I won't keep bashing you. Thanks. I appreciate everything you've put into this. I don't think I've ever had a better birthday than this one."

"I'm tryin' my best, baby. It's your day. All about you."

"Mmm hmm." She rolled her eyes, still smiling wider than Blake could remember her ever smiling before. She took a single rose from the bunch and started up the stairs.

It seemed to Blake like she was swinging her hips a little more than before.

"Stop teasing me like this," he said as he walked up the stairs behind her.

"It's definitely a tease. I just got out the hospital, got stiches and staples all in my arms and shit, my leg got burns and bandages on it. Everything that glitters isn't gold. I look like a monster under this gown."

"Monsters get fucked, too."

"Ol' nasty ass bastard."

"You married this ol' nasty ass bastard."

"Second biggest mistake of my life."

He reached out and grabbed a handful of meaty buttock. She didn't stop or look back, and his hand stayed there until they made it to the master bedroom that the two of them had once shared.

Then she slapped his hand away and went through her walk-in closet to the bathroom.

He fell back onto the oversized bed and grinned up at the ceiling.

He muttered one word.

"Yes!"

Chapter 19

A million thoughts ran through Alexus's mind as she stood at the sink mirror and studied her reflection.

None of them were positive.

She felt that the injuries she'd sustained as a result of the Indianapolis suicide bombing had made her ugly.

She felt that Blake had good reason to be with the women he'd been sleeping with lately. At least they weren't badly injured. They weren't facing the rest of their lives in prison. They weren't lunatic cartel bosses who beheaded people for little to nothing.

Tears formed along her lower eyelids. She had to turn away from the mirror as she undressed and removed the bandages; there were fresh gauze and bandages in her closet.

Her bath water was ready, thanks to mansion staff. Like the toilet, sink, Jacuzzi, and shower, her clawfoot tub was made entirely of white Carrera marble and 24-karat gold.

She went to the bathroom door and locked it and sighed as she submerged herself in the water. Her legs ached from being in one position for so long in the hospital, though according to medical documents, they'd both been routinely stretched to keep them from not working when she was brought out of the coma.

She decided to soak for a while in the soothingly warm water and surf the web and social media on her iPhone.

"Baby, you need some help?" Blake shouted from the bedroom.

"I'm fine," she shouted back. "There's almost a pound of Kush and some blunts in my top drawer. Make yourself at home."

She heard his loveable laugh. Then came the sound of the drawer opening and closing, and the television being turned on.

As usual, she Googled her name first. What came up was a full page of breaking news stories detailing her release from the hospital, her bail and imminent court dates, and her alleged role in the Matamoros Cartel, which authorities now believed was called the Costilla Cartel all throughout Mexico.

Second she Googled her husband's rap name: Bulletface.

There was a TMZ News article centering around Blake's stripper love triangle with Nona Malden, Tasia "Baddie Barbie" Olsen, and Lakita "Bubbles" Thomas. Apparently the three women had engaged in a war of words on Twitter that had all of the Hip Hop community talking.

Next was a Kollege Kidd article about a newly released Bulletface song — "Bodies Everywhere" — that featured his former rival, Chief Keef, and Gucci Mane.

Nothing too fascinating.

Alexus went on to search for news on Blake's thirsty little slut in Atlanta and struck gold.

There had been a second shooting.

She smiled her way through the story and shouted for him when she was done reading, using a thumbnail to flick strands of her long, curly black hair from over her face.

"Yeah?" Blake sounded like he was at the door. "Why you got the door locked?" His voice was moving, and Alexus knew he was going to the second bathroom door at the rear of his own walk-in closet.

Unbeknownst to him, it too was locked.

She heard the doorknob rattle as he tried opening it.

"Haaaa...that's what you on? What if I need to use the bathroom? You gon' lock me out?"

"I don't want you to see me. Trust me, it's brutal. I mean really hideous."

"That's bullshit and you know it." He was back at her bathroom door. "Why in the fuck are you calling me when you got the damn door locked? What kinda sense that make?"

"Did you see the news about your girl Barbie? Somebody came at her again, after the shooting at Lenox Square. Says here that her sister is in critical condition at Emory University Hospital, she was shot in the back with an AK-47. Two policemen died, too. Oh, and the shooter. He was the father of the guy who came for them at the mall. I assume he wanted revenge. Cops intervened. Rest in peace. You know the cycle."

"I bet that shit is hilarious to you."

"One hundred percent!" Alexus said cheerfully. "Any bitch fucking my husband deserves every shred of bad luck that comes her way."

"That wasn't bad luck. You know damned well what that was."

"I honestly couldn't tell you, Blake. I mean, aside from the fact that people are crazy these days. It isn't the first mall shooting in Atlanta. Probably won't be the last."

"You are full of shit. You know you sent them at her."

Alexus gasped jokingly, just loud enough for Blake to hear it. "Sir, are you wearing some kind of recording device?" she asked dramatically. "Because I honestly have no idea who those men were who attacked your lady friend. I only saw it and told you what I've seen on my phone. I've been here in Mexico all day."

She knew he was pissed when he didn't respond. Seconds of silence passed, then the volume on some sports show began blasting in the bedroom.

Alexus snickered wickedly and went on to Google the other two women Blake had been dating. Once she gained all the necessary information on them, she dialed Enrique's mobile number.

He didn't pick up.

A call to Pedro yielded an answer.

"What's going on, little cousin?

"Oh, you know. Same old, same old. Tracking down Blake's bitches and thinking of ways to dispose of them. What's with Gamuza?"

Pedro's chuckle brought back memories of the family's vacation resort and water park in Cancun. There he had laughed day and night as the entire Costilla family had zipped down elaborately built water slides and sky-high rides. He'd always ended up somewhere close to Alexus on the rides. Come to think of it, he'd been closer to her most of her life, and not once had he ever betrayed her. Now, with only him, Alexus, and Mercedes left as the remaining members of the Costilla family, that childhood bond held them together like super glue.

"Gamuza's at a retirement home in Juarez City. He's got his own floor, security all through the place. It'll be a war going in but we can take them with no more than fifteen hundred men. I think it's best if we film the takedown and post it on Liveleak or something. We can wear masks. The most strategic move I believe we can make is for you to behead him on camera. People will automatically think it's you, of course, but no one will know for sure. Just having the other cartels think that it was you is enough, though. It'll shake them to the core knowing that our cartel killed the Zeta's top boss."

"When should I be ready to go after him?" Alexus asked as she ruminated over the idea.

"Tomorrow morning. Doesn't have to be too early but at least make it before noon. We want to get in and get out. Make it look like a military exercise of our men, since the majority of them are Mexican military anyway. We can send in tanks, armored Humvees, fighter jets — the whole nine yards. It'll take us less than twenty minutes, and probably cost you about $100 million, maybe double."

"Money's no issue."

"You don't think I know that?"

"Fine. Let's get to it. I'll call you first thing," Alexus said, gazing vacantly at her red-painted toenails. "Oh, and call off the hits on Blake's little chickenheads for now."

"What's going on with you and him? Did that whole stadium episode just make it all better? Or should I dig his grave like Enrique wants to?"

"Speaking of Enrique, where is he? I just called him."

"On his way to meet Selena at that Hilton hotel down the road. She's that girl he's been on and off with for years. She came into town to see him for the night."

Alexus had heard of the lady on numerous occasions but could not remember ever seeing her. She wondered whether or not she looked better than the woman, and if Enrique would ever consider dumping the woman for her.

Wrong thoughts, she quickly told herself.

"I'm in the tub," Alexus went on. "Call you first thing."

She ended the call and soaped up good before rinsing and standing to step out of the tub. Once her skin was dry and her heavy white robe was on, she applied the doctor prescribed ointments and bandages to her body, added a number of hygiene products to the mix, and walked to the bathroom door.

Opening it, she saw that Blake was lying on the bed in his boxers with the TV remote in hand, smoking a blunt and blowing rings of smoke at the ceiling.

He looked at her. "Evil ass," he said.

"Boy, please. I'm nowhere near evil. You almost got me to that point, I can't even lie, but you know I'm far from that." Alexus got under the covers and pulled them up to her waist as she sat up with her back against the headboard. "Get your ass up."

Blake sat up with her.

"This some good ass weed," he commented as he took a deep pull on the blunt and then regarded it with a serious look as he began coughing so hard that spit flew from his mouth.

Alexus snatched it from between his thumb and forefinger and filled her own lungs with the almost unbearably potent smoke. The blunt went back and forth between them a few times. Playing on the TV was an episode of Brick House of Atlanta, a new show in the Brick House franchise that Alexus's Minority Television Network had brought to the living rooms of millions of Americans just a couple of summers prior with the aid of Trintino "T-Walk" Walkson. It was currently the number-one reality show in all of television, next to two other Brick Houses and the Love and Hip Hop franchise.

This particular episode, the Brick House girls were at an Atlanta Hawks game, and one of them was throwing huge shade over another girl's alleged relationship with a Hawks point guard who'd reportedly filed for bankruptcy last year.

"This shit is hilarious, baby." Blake was fully entertained by the foolishness, probably because all the Brick House girls were Hip Hop video models and urban magazine "booty" models with big butts and pretty faces.

Alexus took the remote and turned the TV off. "Fuck those bitches. We need to have a serious conversation. I have trial coming up soon; tomorrow morning I'll be flying out to Juarez to finally put an end to the Gamuza situation; and I want you to tell me some things, like where do we stand, and how do we get back to the love that we once had. Is that even possible?"

"We couldn't talk all this over with the TV on?" Blake asked.

"No. Your whole attention would be on those bitches."

He grinned at her, then leaned in and kissed her cheek. "Okay. Go right ahead. Talk away."

Alexus sucked her teeth, rolled her eyes, twisted her neck, and hit the blunt again all in one quick motion. "You get on my last nerve, Blake. You really do." Of course she didn't mean it. What she really meant was "I love everything about you, Blake. I really do." But tough love was her kind of love.

"Well, first off," she continued, "I'm getting a tiny chip implanted somewhere under my skin within the next few weeks, so that if I'm convicted it'll be easy to locate me everywhere I am. I'm not going down like that. I'll escape the first time they try putting me in one of those prison vans. I might have to flee the country but I don't care. I've got enough money to do it successfully."

"You're crazy as crazy gets."

"Not true. I'm just not taking any chances. I'm not about to let some judge take my life over some bullcrap information my uncle gave the feds before he was killed."

"I never did like that fat muhfucka."

"Yeah, me neither. But forget him. First thing tomorrow, we're going after the man who beheaded my grandfather, the man my father wanted so badly to catch but never did. I'm doing it for Papi."

"Wait," Blake said, "I thought all the cartels had fallen under your power? Ain't he technically a teammate?"

"Not with the way he sent for you and our kids. No, he's an enemy just like he always was. I don't know why I let my uncle talk me into making that deal in the first place. They just wanted in on my money. They know my submarines have been successfully bringing thousands of kilos here to this country for years now. I'm the prime example of what Pablo Escobar would have been had he continued on doing what he did best, and they knew it. It's okay, though. Lesson learned. I'll never let it happen again. From here on out it's Costilla Cartel or no cartel at all."

Blake nodded his head in agreement. It was then that Alexus realized his hand was rubbing and gently squeezing her right thigh under the covers.

She felt her pussy quiver hungrily and moisten to its peak of wetness.

"Well, I suppose this is the time where you tell me what it's going to be," she said, holding in a moan.

"What it's gon' be? Between us?" He leaned in again, this time to kiss and suck at her earlobe. "You know I'm here for you forever. We might go through our lil beefs here and there, but we're married. I love you. For better or worse, through sickness and health, till death do us part. Remember saying that? I meant it."

Smiling warmly, she reached under the covers and roughly grabbed his wrist. She raised his sneaky little hand from under the covers and kissed its palm.

"Stop it."

"What the fuck you mean 'stop it'? I thought we just went through this? We are married. There's things that come with that. Obligations. I got needs."

"And so do I," Alexus said with a smirk. "Like right now, I 'needs' to take my ass to sleep." She kissed his lips, cut off the lamp on her nightstand, and pulled the covers up to her neck as she slithered down onto her pillows and turned her back to him. "Goodnight, hubby. Sweet dreams."

"Fuck you," Blake barked.

Seconds later she felt his hard dick pressing into her back as he snuggled up close to her, and it made her more horny than she could ever remember being, but she kept her composure and drifted off to sleep.

King Rio

Chapter 20

He wasn't sure how long he'd been asleep when he woke with a full bladder.

Alexus was out cold. He kissed her on the neck, his eyes shutting as he took in her alluring Clive Christian perfume, and got up to use the bathroom, picking up his iPhone from the charging pad along the way. He'd locked it before setting it there, so as not to expose the many texts and pictures Nona, Bubbles, and Barbie had sent him over the past few weeks. He knew it would probably result in Alexus ordering yet another hit, and that was something he was trying to avoid.

Pissing and yawning, he checked his notifications. There were four new voicemails; two new text messages from Barbie, one from his brother, Streets, and none from Nona or Bubbles.

Thinking about it, he had to laugh once. He knew exactly why Nona and Bubbles hadn't messaged him. They were both utterly afraid of Alexus, and knowing that he'd left to be with her, they weren't taking any chances with messages that Alexus might possibly read.

He flushed the toilet and decided to listen to the voicemail messages while he reentered the bedroom and went in his duffle bag for his stack of Styrofoam cups, a 20-ounce bottle of Sprite, and a pint of Promethazine with Codeine syrup. All he needed now was ice, and he was grateful for the miniature fridge on Alexus's side of the bed that stayed stocked full of ice and beverages

This was the kind of night when he usually woke up and made rough thug love to Nona or Bubbles. Here lately they'd both been sleeping in the same bed with him.

He stood at the foot of the bed and read Barbie's texts first.

'Can u PLEASE tell your girl to FALL THE FUCK BACK! Okay, I give! Fuck u SHE CAN HAVE U! I got MAD love for u an all but its not worth dying over! My sister's n the hospital on life support! Tf yo! Is this why your name's Bulletface! I'm done! D.O.N.E.!'

'Answer Ur Phone!'

Of course he'd had the phone on airplane mode the entire time he'd been with Alexus, merely to avoid more drama with wifey. She was already on him enough. He figured Alexus seeing a text from another woman definitely would not have led to him sleeping in bed with her.

He listened to the voicemail messages while scooping a cup into the box of ice in the short refrigerator. One of them was from around the time his flight was landing in Matamoros, and the others were from just under an hour ago.

"Oh, my God, Blake! What the fuck is up with your bitch? Me and my people just had to literally kill someone in self-defense because of that fucking psycho you're married to! You can tell that bitch right now that I'm not playing with her at all. Every motherfucker she sends my way will get the same treatment her little friend just got. Call me when you get this message. I'll probably be leaving Lenox Square by then."

There was a clear shift in Barbie's attitude from the very beginning of the next voicemail:

"I'm sorry, okay? Tell her I'm sorry! I shouldn't be fucking a married man in the first place. I'm changing my number and moving the fuck away from here, okay? Please tell her to call off these crazy Mexicans. My sister's in the intensive care unit with a hole through her back and chest. She might not fucking make it!"

Barbie hung up abruptly. Blake glanced over at Alexus as she turned over onto her other side. He mixed up the Sprite and medicinal syrup then poured it over his cup of ice and pressed play on the next voicemail.

Barbie was sobbing now:

"You should fly me away somewhere, Blake. Get me away. I'm terrified. I don't know what to do. If they found me here they might find me anywhere in this" —she sniffled and blew her nose— "fucked up city. Send me to another country with enough to live on...I'm scared, okay? I take back everything I said before, alright? Please, Blake... Get whoever's after me to stop."

Blake didn't want to hear anymore. He deleted the messages and sat down next to Alexus. Almost immediately, she turned over again. Her eyes fluttered open a crack. She smiled sleepily.

"You might want to turn the volume down on your phone. I heard that bitch crying and complaining."

Glad to see her awake, Blake kissed Alexus's lips twice and slipped a hand under the cover to squeeze and rub her ass. This time there was no resistance. Her sleepy little smirk grew into a full-on smile. Her eyes opened wider.

"I'm hungry, baby," he said, knowing that his meaning of hungry would instantly register in her mind.

As it did. She turned onto her back, pushing the covers aside, and parted her legs.

"I have to be somewhere in the morning, so make it quick," she said, adjusting the silk Louis Vuitton pillows under her head.

Blake's wandering hand moved between Alexus's thick thighs as he turned up his cup for a swallow of his special drink.

"I don't know why they call that Lean," Alexus said in the groggiest of tones. "Looks to me like it's making you fatter, not leaner."

Blake laughed and put his cup and phone on Alexus's nightstand. For the first time he noticed that her whole left leg was wrapped in gauze and bandages, but he hardly gave them a glance as he got on the bed and buried his face between her thighs.

It seemed like a lifetime had passed since he'd last tasted her.

He went straight for her clitoris and sucked mercilessly, shoving his middle finger in and out of her juicy opening.

His dick quickly swelled to a full erection.

He did his usual move — holding her clit in his mouth while sucking, licking, and swishing saliva around it. She held his head in her hands and grinded her hips upward, moaning a steady "Mmmm...mmmm..." and occasionally yelping in pleasure.

He'd hardly been going for a minute when her juices started squirting out. He got up on his knees and rapidly rubbed his fingertips on her clit as her stream of juices continued to gush out.

Then he pushed down his boxers and wrapped a hand around the base of his thick twelve-inch phallus.

He was easing forward, getting ready to impale her, when she slammed her legs shut and rolled over on her side.

"Thanks," she said with a tired giggle as she closed her eyes. "Goodnight."

"Wait...what?"

"You heard me. Did you honestly think it would be that easy to fuck me after all the rotten pussies you've been fucking? Ha! Yeah, right. Goodnight, Blake."

The right side of Blake's mouth rose in a snarl of discontent. He tried to slide in his dick between her thighs and was quickly shoved away.

"Bitch," he mumbled, frustrated.

He jerked his erection for a few minutes, until it shot ropes of semen all over Alexus's exposed butt cheek.

Then he lay beside her with his back to her and grinned as he felt Alexus moving around next to him. He knew she was wiping off his cum.

"Asshole," she murmured.

"Bitch," he repeated, under his breath.

Chapter 21

A mile away from the Matamoros mansion, Enrique lay awake in bed in his penthouse suite at the Hilton hotel.

His lady friend, Selena, was fast asleep next to him. The two of them had two daughters together (a fact he hadn't known for certain until a recent DNA test had proved it). They'd been dating on and off for years, but Enrique had kept the relationship a secret from everyone, including the Costilla family. The cartel life was much too dangerous. He'd lost so many men to cartel wars that he feared he'd also lose Selena if ever their relationship was revealed, and that was a risk he did not want to take.

He slipped out of bed, nude except for the pair of socks on his feet, and walked to the large window that overlooked the city's bustling downtown area.

It was ten minutes past two o'clock in the morning.

Stars were twinkling in the black sky. Cars and trucks and motorcycles, as tiny as insects, were zipping around on the streets below. It was a soothing sight to Enrique. It made him think of how life would be if and when he ever left the Costilla Cartel and settled down with his dear lady friend.

He tried without success to shake away the thought that had been troubling him for hours now.

The kiss he'd gotten from Alexus Costilla.

He knew he'd always been attracted to the beautiful Black-and-Mexican bombshell, but never had he thought she felt the same way.

Not until the kiss.

Now, he was rethinking all the times he remembered being around her and sensing an odd sexual tension. It had occurred several times over the years, but neither he nor Alexus had ever made a move. There were times when he'd been tempted to approach her back when her father was still alive, but he'd known that such a mistake could have easily led to his own gruesome beheading. Papi hadn't played about his daughter. When Enrique first started as personal bodyguard and head of security for Vida Costilla, Alexus's deceased grandmother, he'd been taught to keep his hands and eyes off the future cartel boss. Then she'd only been 16.

She was 23 now, a grown woman with a kid and a burgeoning entertainment corporation. She could make her own decisions. If she wanted to date him, there would be no repercussions. Alexus Costilla was essentially the most important woman in the world. In fact, she'd recently been named "The world's most powerful woman" by Forbes Magazine. She owned television networks, a vacation resort in Cancun, and millions of shares in some of the stock market's most lucrative businesses.

Enrique closed his eyes until the lustful thoughts escaped him. He couldn't date Alexus. He was her bodyguard and head of security. His job was to protect her, not strike up a relationship. Plus, she was married.

"Married to a flashy fucking gangster rapper," he whispered aloud to himself. "He's just like those other rap guys. It's all about the bling and the Bugattis, the fucking women. I bet he's bedded a thousand whores. I know it."

He liked Blake, but only on a man-to-man, mutual respect kind of level. He didn't respect the way Blake lived. He didn't respect the way Blake treated women, especially since Blake had a daughter who needed a good father figure. He also didn't respect how Blake flaunted the cartel's drug money in strip clubs and at parties with his music industry friends. He was surprised that the feds had yet to connect Blake to the cartel, though he suspected they already knew and were merely biding their time before bringing down indictments on him and his gang.

Enrique's ruminations were interrupted by the ringing of his smartphone. He rushed to it so as not to awaken Selena.

She stirred but remained in dreamland.

The call was from one of the Costilla Cartel's men in Chicago.

Enrique always took calls when he was woke, Even if it was in the middle of the night when he was only up for a quick piss.

He answered. "Yeah?"

"We've located the two girls in Chicago. They're together at a strip club at the moment. Should we take them or end them?"

Enrique became thoughtful. He was back at the window, this time gazing at the lights in the windows of the Marriott hotel across the street.

He tried to remember Alexus's last orders on the women Blake had cheated on her with, Nona and Bubbles.

Then he said forget it and gave the order.

"Go ahead and take them. If the boss says end them, I'll tell you. Keep them alive until then."

When Enrique returned to bed, there was a huge smile on his handsome brown face.

He draped an arm over Selena and was asleep seconds later.

King Rio

Chapter 22

"That nigga Cup is so damn smart. Look at all that money. This shit makes me wanna go back to dancing here. If Blake's ass wasn't looking out for us the way he is I'd be right back on that pole." Bubbles was as serious as a heart attack.

She and Nona were posted up at the bar inside Redbone's, a strip club on the corner of 16th and Trumbull Avenue in Chicago's Lawndale neighborhood. They were waiting on another round of shots. Their eyes were on all the dollars that were raining down on two young strippers who were clapping their asses and swinging around the poles onstage while King Louie and his entourage performed on a separate stage.

Chicago rappers Sicko Mobb, Katie Got Bandz, and Lil Herb were also in the building. They were in the VIP section with five more stunning young strippers.

The club was packed with over a thousand Chicagoans, which wasn't the club's full capacity but still much more than Redbone's got on most Tuesday nights.

"I bet this muhfucka would be filled from wall to wall if Blake was here," Nona said.

"You know it would," Bubbles agreed.

"That nigga would be throwin' all hundreds. Fuck some ones."

"And he would've bought everybody bottles as soon as he walked in the door."

"Look at how these bitches lookin' at us. They too mad." The bartender came with their shots, and Nona immediately tossed one back.

Bubbles gulped down her shot. The tequila played like a flamethrower in her throat. "You know these hoes hate seeing us in here in red bottoms and thirty-thousand-dollar Gucci dresses."

"All white everything, too? Bitch, we the shit."

Nona was referring to the snug white dresses she and Bubbles had on. She was feeling herself. They were at the bar buying shots when they could have easily dropped thousands of dollars on bottles.

They took shots until they were nice and tipsy, chatting about every man and woman they saw.

That was, until Mercedes Costilla and her sister Porsche entered the club with a group of twenty more people, all of whom were wearing all black outfits and shoes.

"Tell me my eyes are playing tricks on me," Bubbles said as she and everyone else watched the mob of black-attired men and women headed up to VIP. "Ain't that Alexus?"

"No, that's Mercedes," Nona said. "They look a lot alike but you can tell the difference. For one, Alexus only wears white."

"Oh, forgot about that."

"Mmm hmm. And Mercedes been wearing all black for a while now. She's from here on the west side Chicago. Look at all the people shouting at her. She knows everybody. That's her sister walking behind her."

"Damn, that is Porsche. That dirty bitch drugged Blake and recorded herself sucking his dick. They should've killed her when they shot her ass in Barbados."

"Come on, let's go up there," Nona said, and headed off toward the stairs that led up to the VIP rooms.

She had to swat a few hands down and shout some cuss words as a couple thirsty young niggas tried groping her and Bubbles.

With them both being known all over as two of Bulletface's lovers, they had no problem joining the VIP guests. As soon as Mercedes saw them she waved them over and offered them each a bottle of Dom.

"The hell y'all doin' up in here?" Bubbles asked.

"Sis ain't been out for a good time since she got out the hospital," Porsche answered. "We all decided to come here to see King Louie's performance. Well, she did. I just came to see Katie."

Mercedes said hello to Nona and Bubbles and then asked the question that Nona was half-expecting. "Y'all still messing around with Blake?"

"Not since Alexus is home," Nona said, eyeing the black diamonds in Mercedes's tennis bracelet and Michael Kors watch. "I think he's in Mexico with her. Or wherever she went. What is up with you and all this black? Are you gonna wear black the way Alexus wears white?"

"Nona." Mercedes took a deep breath before continuing. "I've lost my entire family fucking with that damn...Costilla family. All I have left is Porsche. I'll be in mourning until the day I die, so I'll wear black until that day comes. You understand?"

Nona did not understand but she nodded and said she did, if only to end the painfully disheartening conversation.

The bottles started flowing and the blunts started burning. Soon they were all cheering on the strippers and throwing fistfuls of dollars in the air. Mercedes was nowhere near as wealthy as Alexus but her money was long. She bought a hundred bottles of Dom and had eighty of them passed out to the less fortunate. She threw $30,000 in singles at the strippers. She stood up and swayed her hips a little. Nona and Bubbles got loose and twerked in their tight dresses, taking the shine from the other strippers who weren't as thick where it counted.

The turn up was real.

In fact, the girls had so much fun together that Mercedes invited them to join her and her crew at their Sybaris Hotel suite when they were all ready to leave.

Everyone in VIP agreed to go.

"I thought this night was gon' end with us watching Netflix at Blake's mansion," Nona said to Bubbles as they were leaving out the side door of Redbone's.

"Nuh uh, bitch." Bubbles was as happy as can be. "We turnin' up tonight."

A few guys from Mercedes and Porsche's group made small talk with Nona and Bubbles as they traversed the parking lot to where Nona's brand-new 2016 Range Rover (a gift from Blake) was parked. They were both intoxicated but Bubbles agreed to drive. She'd done a lot of tipsy driving whenever they went out when Blake wasn't in town.

Once seated comfortably in the luxury SUV, they put on their seatbelts and looked at the two blacked out Mercedes Maybachs and four equally black Escalades that Mercedes Costilla's crew were all getting into.

Random people were stopping Mercedes to take pictures, while others were snapping pics from afar and recording video.

"That bitch is so lucky to be related to Alexus," Nona said, her voice slurring as Bubbles turned the key in the ignition. "It's a good thing, though, you know. She was born and raised in a poor household, didn't find out Alexus was her sister until she was already eighteen. I mean, it hasn't been all sweet, with her losing her family and all, but at least she's set for life now. She'll never have to work another job share again."

"If we can get some babies out of Blake we'll be the same way." Bubbles had a point.

"Yeah, if we can get the nigga to stop wearing condoms. The fuck is up with that shit?"

"It might be a good thing for now. Alexus is going hard on Barbie. Or at least that's what Barbie says. We might wanna wait until the judge locks Alexus up and throws away the key. Then Blake will be ours for the taking."

Barbie had called Bubbles and told her everything there was to know about the Atlanta shootings. The news made her and Nona glad that Blake had left to be with Alexus. Maybe it would keep the crazy billionaire off their heels.

Bubbles followed Mercedes's fleet of sparkling black vehicles out of the parking lot and down 16th Street. Nona upped the volume on the album her brother Biggs had recently dropped. It was titled "Already Rich" and featured some of the hottest names in Hip Hop, including Bulletface.

They had just turned onto Roosevelt Road when a police car appeared behind them with its lights flashing.

"You've gotta be fucking kidding me," Bubbles said, adjusting the rearview mirror to look at the cop car.

Nona dug in her Birkin bag for the quarter ounce of Kush she'd brought to the club with her and quickly stuffed it in her pussy as Bubbles pulled over.

Mercedes and her crew kept going and made a left turn at the next traffic light.

"Don't look suspicious," Bubbles said, eyes wide — looking suspicious.

They watched through the sideview and rearview mirrors as two policemen got out of the squad car with their guns aimed at the Range Rover.

"What the fuck do they have guns aimed at us for?!" Nona said incredulously.

"Get out of the car! Now!" shouted one policeman.

Bubbles and Nona pushed open their doors and stepped out with their hands raised high above their heads.

The policemen approached swiftly and cuffed their hands behind their backs.

Nona studied the faces of the policemen as they pulled her and Nona toward the squad car.

They were Hispanic men with cold, beady eyes.

"What did we do?" Bubbles asked.

"I know my fucking rights," Nona said.

"Both of you shut up," said the slimmer of the two policemen.

Which is when Nona noticed the bloody handprint on the driver's door of the CPD car, and five bullet holes near the keyhole.

It struck her then.

Something wasn't right. In fact, something was terribly wrong, and Nona immediately guessed that Alexus Costilla was behind that something.

As she was shoved against the blood-smeared door, she shut her eyes and prayed to God for safety.

When she opened her eyes, Mercedes's motorcade of flashy black whips was pulling up alongside the squad car.

Seconds later, Mercedes was out of her Maybach and standing with her hands on her hips, staring the officers down just as they were pulling open the rear doors to put Nona and Bubbles inside.

"These are my friends. What the fuck are you manhandling them for?" Mercedes said.

Nona happened to glance at the floor space in front of the backseats of the squad car, and what she saw made her cringe.

There were two severed heads with bloody, jagged ridges along their necks where whatever kind of knife used to sever them from their shoulders had sawed through. One head belonged to a black man, the other to a white man.

Suddenly Nona wasn't as intoxicated as she'd been moments earlier.

She looked over her shoulder at Mercedes, who's presence seemed to startle the policemen.

"We were told to...to take them," the slim officer said to Mercedes. "Enrique told us to take them. What are you doing here?"

Mercedes paused. Her expression became thoughtful. "Take those cuffs off them right goddamn now. I'll deal with Enrique."

The policemen began talking in Spanish as they removed the handcuffs from Bubbles and Nona's wrists.

The two frightened women moved hastily back to their seats in the Range Rover.

"Did you see those chopped off heads?" Bubbles asked.

"Just drive," Nona said. "Get us the fuck away from here."

Chapter 23

"...Baby, I know you hear me. Wake up, Blake. Get up."

Blake King was being rocked awake by a persistent hand on his left rib.

Reluctantly, he forced his left eyelid to open half an inch, and when he saw that the hand was his wife's he remembered where he was.

"Look at the news, baby! That's in Chicago." She laughed. "You'd think things like this only happened in Mexico."

The sheer joy of waking up in bed with Alexus brought a grateful smile to Blake's face as he sat up, yawning and stretching his strong black arms over his head and turning his attention to the TV. Alexus smelled like she'd just taken another bath and freshened up. She was sitting Indian-style beside him and had on a white T-shirt over baggy white sweatpants.

The caption at the bottom of the screen told Blake all he needed to know:

TWO CHICAGO POLICE OFFICERS FOUND BE-HEADED OVERNIGHT

"The fuck...?" He yawned again.

"I know, crazy as shit, right?"

A gaseous swell in Blake's stomach led to a thunderous roar that vibrated the bed and made Alexus hop up in disgust.

"You are so incredibly trifling," she said, pinching her nostrils shut. "Go in the bathroom and get yourself together, would you? Nasty bastard."

"You married this nasty bastard."

"Shut up and go. Yuck."

He chuckled and grinned his blinging grin. His first instinct was to call Bubbles to check on her and Nona but he thought better of it and got up to use the bathroom.

Alexus saw that his dick was as hard as a flagpole in his Versace boxers and cracked up laughing.

"Don't laugh at this shit. 'Cause you know whose fault it is." Blake wasn't surprised to see Alexus trailing him into the bathroom. He could tell she missed him just as much as he missed her. "Why are you following me if I'm so 'yuck'? That makes a while lotta sense."

"Oh, hush." She sat on the edge of the Jacuzzi and stared wantonly at his erection as he tried to pee.

"Stop looking at me, you fuckin' pervert."

"That's mine, nigga. I can look all I please. Hurry up. We gotta be out of here in the next half hour."

"The kids woke?"

"They're eating breakfast with Momma."

Blake waited and waited for his erection to weaken; he couldn't urinate with an erection.

It wouldn't go away.

"See what the fuck you did?" He cast an accusatory glare at Alexus. "I can't piss with my dick like this. This muhfucka won't even go down."

Alexus rolled her eyes. "Come over here."

Walking to her with his twelve-inch pole dangling over his boxers, Blake tried to keep an upset expression on his face, but his grin broke through.

Alexus grabbed his engorged phallus in both hands, spit on it, and started stroking it tightly.

"You can do way more than that," Blake said, but Alexus ignored him and kept jerking and spitting on his morning wood.

Seconds later she looked up at him and said, "Tell me before you're gonna shoot that gunk out."

He wore a full grin now, and he was pumping his hips forward at her every stroke.

"We're going to Juarez for an important mission this morning," she said. "The guy who beheaded my grandfather is there. We're gonna get him."

"I'm not in that shit."

"Oh, yes you are. Don't forget, you're still technically the boss until I'm back in play."

"How? I thought it was until you got out the hospital?"

She shook her head. "It's until I'm all the way healed."

"You need to stop bullshittin' and put this muhfucka in ya mouth."

Alexus gave another roll of the eyes. "As I was saying, we're going after Gamuza. They made us look bad when they came for you a few weeks ago. We can't allow that to pass without retaliation. We'll have plenty of backup. The military is on our side. It may cost me a few hundred million but I wouldn't care if it cost me a billion. We've gotta get him out of the way before something like that happens again. Once that's over, we might go on this cruise Britney and Melz have been planning. I'll rent out the cruise ship so that it'll only be our people on it with us. Maybe you can invite some of your artists and celebrity friends."

"Mm hmm."

"Are you even listening to me?"

"Yeah. Just keep goin'."

Alexus rolled her eyes for the third time and continued her snug-handed strokes.

"I'm thinking about inviting the girls from my network's reality shows. That'll guarantee some drama to keep us entertained. As long as neither of those bitches throws any drinks my way we'll be fine. 'Cause I'll have a bitch thrown overboard in a heartbeat."

"Invite Thunder," Blake said. It was the only thought that could make it out of his mouth.

"You would want me to invite that bitch," Alexus snapped, squeezing his meat tighter in her hands. "She hasn't spoken to me since T-Walk's funeral. I might just do that. Maybe I'll have my own reality show drama. Who knows. I wouldn't even have my bodyguards jump in if I got in a fight with that bitch. I'd just beat her ass for—"

Alexus gasped and shoved Blake away from her as a thick string of cum shot out and hit her square in the eye.

"You stupid fuck!" she exclaimed.

Chuckling to himself, Blake took control and stroked the rest of the semen out of his twitching penis, while Alexus went to the sink to clean off her face.

By the time she turned back to him, he was at the toilet, smiling broadly as a stream of urine splashed into the toilet's water.

Chapter 24

Alexus's private jet was gassed up and ready. She left the mansion with Enrique, Pedro, Mary, Blake, and a swarm of armed Costilla Cartel militants dressed like federal agents in bulletproof vests and toting sidearms and assault rifles.

On the plane, she went over the plot to murder Gamuza with Pedro and Enrique, speaking in Spanish to keep Mary out of the business, while Blake smoked blunts and sipped Lean.

The plan was simple. Her men, alongside the Mexican military, would surround the building where Gamuza was hiding out and order everyone out. Those who resisted would be killed. Those who did not resist would be handcuffed and taken to a remote area in southern Juarez. There they would be brutally beheaded and buried in shallow graves. Their heads would be delivered to the doorsteps of their closest relatives.

Gamuza was the ultimate prize to the Costilla family. He was to be beheaded with a chainsaw by Alexus Costilla, in the same way that he'd killed her grandfather.

All throughout the tense conversation, Alexus kept glancing across the aisle at Blake. He had the sexiest swag she'd ever seen a man possess, and the fact that it was an effortless swag made him even more irresistible. He had on essentially the same all-white outfit she did: white jeans and a shirt, Louboutin sneakers, a Hublot watch and a brown diamond-encrusted Jesus pendant hanging from his gold necklace. Only his jeans were loose-fitting and hers were tight, and he had on Louis Vuitton sunglasses, while hers were Chanel.

The sound of her cousin Pedro raising his voice shook Alexus from her reverie.

"Alexus, will you pay attention to what I'm saying here? It's quite important, believe it or not," Pedro said, obviously irritated that she'd missed what he'd said. "He'll be right here on this plane when we're done talking."

She smiled. "If he's not it's a trick to it."

"As I was saying," Pedro went on, "the United States government has revoked our diplomatic immunity, so be careful when you return to the States. They can pull us over and disregard those cards. They can search us, arrest us; we'll have to pay taxes from here on out."

"Taxes!" Alexus was shocked.

"Yeah. We're basically just like the rest of America now."

"What made them change up on us like this?" Alexus asked, taking a drink of water and clicking on her iPhone screen to see the time. "I thought that was permanent?"

Enrique shook his head. Today he and Pedro wore white Hartmarx suits, the brand that had at one time been worn by all members of the Costilla Cartel.

"If you would have taken your spot on the Counsel, we wouldn't be going through any of this. This is their way of saying fuck you for not joining."

Alexus pressed the edge of her iPhone to her chin, thinking. She'd turned down the government's offer for a very good reason. They had essentially wanted her to become a leader of the main branch of the Illuminati. Enrique had told her all about it, and once she'd given it some thought, she'd chosen to go her own route and just run her corporation the way she wanted to, with little to no help from the U.S. government. Her mother had an MBA from Harvard, and with Britney Bostic's law firm on the team with them, Alexus knew her corporation would thrive through even the toughest of economic times. Costilla Corporation was trading at $192.77 a share, nearly double what Time Warner shares were going for. She knew that her competitors were praying for her fall from the top, but it seemed like nothing — not even her current legal troubles and the allegations of her being the head of Mexico's deadliest drug cartel — could stop the stock traders from investing in the gold mine that was Costilla Corp.

She briefly wondered if it would all go down the drain if she happened to be convicted of the federal charges she was now facing.

She prayed that it would not, if only for the sake of King Neal and Savaria's futures. As long as the kids were guaranteed a financially stable future, Alexus was okay with however things turned out.

She kept the smartphone pressed deep in the middle of her chin as she turned to her window and stared out into the clouds. Her mind wandered. The fear of dying in Mexico was heavy in her gut. She thought that maybe this Gamuza mission was a trap. He'd survived over sixty years being hunted by not only the Costilla Cartel, but also the Gulf and Sinaloa cartels and numerous Mexican and American federal police agencies, and not once had he been captured.

Alexus's heart pounded in her chest. She glanced at Blake again, this time searching for the emotional support that she needed.

As if reading her mind, he got up and canted his head toward the restroom, motioning for her to follow him there. He went first, and she joined him a moment later.

When she walked in the restroom, he was leaned back with his hands on the sink. He looked at her and said, "What's wrong?"

Alexus shut and locked the door. "What made you say that?"

"The look on your face. I've known you long enough to know when something's bothering you."

She stepped in front of him, a growing smile on her face, and pressed her lips to his. "You know me so well."

"I know I do. So," he said, putting his arms around her waist and his hands in the back pockets of her jeans, "tell me what's wrong."

"It's nothing really." She laid her head on his chest. "All this killing might just be getting to me. I'm worried that something might go wrong in Juarez. It seems too easy to me. We've been after Gamuza forever. My grandmother had a thousand men go to Juarez to look for him when I was fifteen. Most of them were killed. The rest went missing."

"All of em?"

Alexus nodded. "See what I mean? It's too hard to catch him. He has control over all of Juarez."

"Well, how do you think Flako was able to reach him? Didn't they have some kind of meeting?"

"Yeah. No one knows how Flako got to him. The Zetas are far too loyal to give him up, and the residents are too afraid. Even the police are afraid."

Blake shook his head and let out a breath. "We'll figure it out. Just relax. You might need to smoke a lil bit of that loud pack I got. All this stressing ain't gon' get you nowhere. Shit, we're halfway there now. Ain't no lookin' back. Time to push forward and implement whatever plan y'all got. I'm with it."

Alexus pulled back and stared at Blake's ridiculously handsome dark face. She put the tip of a forefinger on his chin and tilted his head down for a kiss. He leaned forward with no hesitation, and their lips connected.

The kiss ignited a fire in Alexus's nether regions. It was a kiss that could have easily lasted until the end of their flight and she would not have had a single complaint.

For a long while they kept their lips locked, tongue-kissing and sucking on each other's bottom lips, squeezing and rubbing and touching. Alexus tasted the Kush and Lean in his mouth, and she didn't mind. She felt his phallus grow hard against her stomach. The inclination to undo his Louis Vuitton belt and service him came to her, but she had a better idea.

Pulling back, she said, "I want you inside me."

"You ain't said nothin' but a word." Blake grinned.

"You got a condom?"

"Fuck I need a condom for?"

"Umm...maybe because you've been fucking your sluts all month long."

"I wore condoms every time."

"Never mind," Alexus said, suddenly pissed at the thought of Blake fucking other women. She unlocked the door and snatched it open. "Jerk yourself this time."

"Ain't this a bitch..." she heard Blake saying as she left out and swung the door shut behind her.

As she was walking past Enrique, he said, "Got a call from our guys in Chicago last night. They had those two girls, but Mercedes happened to be there with them. She told them to let the girls go."

"Call them back and ask them if they work for me or my sister. I said I want those bitches dead, and that's what it's going to be," Alexus said through clenched teeth.

Instead of rejoining Pedro and Enrique, she went to the seat next to Mary, two rows behind Blake's seat.

"I hate men," Alexus muttered.

"I can't believe I'm sitting next to Alexus Costilla," Mary said with a giggle.

Alexus gave no reply.

King Rio

Chapter 25

When Mercedes Costilla woke up and looked around, she saw that her Sybaris hotel suite resembled the beginning of a Hangover movie, and she wondered if she'd encounter a tiger in the bathroom when she went to pee.

Thankfully, she did not run into a wild feline, but there was a half-naked girl lying in the middle of the floor that she had to step over to make it to the toilet.

The girl was still there when she left the bathroom minutes later.

She paused and looked around the room.

Empty bottles of Remy and Hennessy littered the floor. A glass table was broken, and there was blood on the shattered glass. Porsche and her underaged friend Sasha were wrapped in each other's arms on the sofa. Someone's bra was floating in the swimming pool.

Bubbles and Nona were up already; they were sitting in the Jacuzzi, passing a blunt back and forth and whispering about something.

The others who'd joined them last night were in other suites.

"They fucked up my room and went to theirs to go to sleep. Dirty ass niggas," Mercedes said.

Bubbles looked back at her. "You got a gun? Preferably a big one?"

"For real," Nona added as she stood and stepped out of the Jacuzzi, wrapping a towel around her waist. "That move last night has me terrified. I called Biggs. Him and Meach are way out in New Jersey. They had a concert there last night. He said he'll be here in a few hours."

"Well," Mercedes said, picking up her black croc skin Birkin bag and checking it to see if anything had been stolen while she was sleeping, "I don't want any of Blake's people around me period, so make sure y'all ain't here when you meet up with them. I'm done fucking with him and Alexus. You see what happened last night. Those motherfuckers are beyond crazy, and I ain't got time for it. Alexus had my momma killed on accident, Blake had my baby daddy killed, and my kids were killed by that Jenny Costilla. I hate my last name is even Costilla. I'm about to change that shit to my mom's last name."

"Do you think you can follow us to Blake's mansion first?" Bubbles asked as she too stepped out of the Jacuzzi. "Just so we can get our stuff. I'm about to go pick up my daughter and fly out to New York. I think I'm done with Blake's ass, too. At least until they lock Alexus up. I'm not about to lose my life because of some nigga."

"Me, neither," Nona said. "That shit is all over the news. Says they ambushed two real police officers and killed them to take their uniforms. I can't understand why they cut off those officers' heads. That was so uncalled for. Those men have families."

"It's the Costilla Cartel. What did you expect?" Mercedes went to the sofa and woke up Porsche and Sasha. "Y'all get up so we can go. Look at that damn table. Hope y'all don't think I'm paying for that shit."

"You're the one who broke it," Nona said. "When you pushed that girl last night. She fell right through it."

Mercedes frowned. "I pushed a girl? What girl?"

"Tara," Porsche said sleepily.

Mercedes gasped as the memory came to her. She and Tara, a childhood friend of hers, had started arguing because Tara had once slept with the deceased father of Mercedes's deceased children. Mercedes had grabbed Tara by the hair and thrown her into the table.

She laughed once. "Damn. I did do that, huh?" She shook her head in disbelief.

Tara had been a part of the twenty people Mercedes had taken with her to the strip club. They were all originally from the rundown apartment building on the corner of Lake and Lockwood where Mercedes and Porsche were born and raised. Ever since she was released from the Los Angeles hospital, Mercedes had been keeping her old friends around, mainly because the girls were rowdy and the guys were all gang members who toted guns on the regular. She'd bought the Escalades for them and the second Maybach for Porsche, all paid for by the $7.4 million she'd inherited from her father — deceased Mexican drug lord Juan Costilla. She'd used some of the money to get them all situated in new homes. She'd given them all $25,000 apiece. She'd even purchased a hundred pounds of high-grade marijuana for them to package up and give to younger gang members to distribute, all to build up her own team, a team that could defend her from the Costilla Cartel and all its enemies, as well as all the threats other Chicago gangs posed to her and her crew.

One of the most important of her purchases was a shipment of guns. Handguns, assault rifles, and shotguns. $30,000 to an Indiana gun dealer had gotten her all the weapons she and her crew needed.

She had a 9-millimeter Ruger and a 30-shot clip in her bag. She took it out and showed it to Nona.

"No worries," she said.

"I'm still worried," Nona said.

"Yeah, me too," Bubbles said. "Can you please call Alexus and get her to give whatever order she needs to give to cancel the hit they have on us?"

"No." Mercedes picked up a Hennessy bottle from the floor and tossed it in the trash. "I told you, I'm not calling Alexus. Not today, not tomorrow, not ever. I don't know that girl in the first place. I'm from Chicago. She's from Texas. Didn't meet her until I was already grown, and even though I was struggling like hell then, I'd go back to that any day. I would much rather be dead broke with a family to feed than rich with a dead family."

Nona and Bubbles must have felt her pain, because they got quiet and helped clean up a bit before breakfast arrived.

As Mercedes was eating her usual omelette with cheese and green peppers, she went on Twitter to see what her mentions were looking like. She still had nine million followers, the same as she'd had before going to the hospital. Most of her mentions were from concerned fans wishing her well and welcoming her home from the hospital, though she'd been home for a few days now.

She posted a tweet:

'Thanks Every1 for the well wishes! I love you all...'

"I need to start some kind of business," she said thoughtfully. "With all these followers I have, I could be making millions."

Porsche nodded. "Like the Kardashians."

"No, like me," Mercedes said. "I think I'm going to reach back out to some of those companies that have been offering to pay me to promote their products. Not now, though. When all these scars and bruises heal up."

She hadn't been hurt as badly as Alexus in the Indianapolis hotel blast, but she still had stitches in her side and more in her left wrist. Shrapnel injuries mostly. She would be fine in due time. The wounds ached a little every now and then, but she took more than enough pills to deal with the pain.

She told Porsche and Sasha to have their pistols cocked and their purses open before they left out; there was no telling if Alexus's men would return in search of Nona and Bubbles.

Once Mercedes got all her friends up, they left the hotel in a hurry and headed for Blake's mansion.

Mercedes sat alone in the backseat of her Maybach. Shakema, her big-boned friend who'd lived across the hall from her in the building on Lockwood, was her driver.

"Girl," Shakema said, "did you see what went down with those police officers last night?"

"Yeah, I heard." Now Mercedes was on Instagram, posting a picture she'd taken of the broken table. She added the caption: "Crazy night with the woes. #BitchHadMeFuckedUp #GotThrown-ThroughAGlassTable". A demon emoji sealed the deal, and she uploaded the photo.

Just then, she glanced out her back window and saw a man on a dirtbike zooming his way through traffic.

The man had a gun with a silencer in his left hand.

Acting on instinct, she pushed open her door just as the dirtbike was about to pass.

The front wheel hit her door and sent the driver flying over it. His helmet struck the ground so hard that a large portion of it broke off and skittered away with the man's pistol.

"What the fuck...?" Shakema exclaimed.

"Stop the car." Mercedes drew her gun and waited for the half-million-dollar car to come to a halt.

They were on North Avenue, a fairly busy west side street.

Onlookers gawked in shock at the grounded motorcyclist as Mercedes approached him.

He was on his side, a ribbon of blood pouring out of his mouth. His eyes were moving, but nothing else was.

"You're with the Costilla Cartel, aren't you?" Mercedes asked knowingly.

"The queen...the queen's orders..."

The five words were the man's last words, and not as a result of his injuries.

His death was caused by the single round Mercedes fired from her Ruger pistol.

The man's head cracked open like an egg.

"Fuck the Costilla Cartel," Mercedes muttered as she got back in the car with her now frightened friend.

"Girl, you just shot that man!" Shakema's hands were shaking on the steering wheel.

"What am I paying you to do?" Mercedes snapped. "Drive!"

King Rio

Chapter 26

Alexus Costilla faced an immediate problem when her plane landed in Juarez.

Enrique informed her that somehow the paparazzi had gotten word of her imminent arrival, and now more than twenty men and women with cameras were waiting for her in the airport.

The news infuriated Alexus, who knew that this was the wrong time for cameras to be snapping her pictures. She was here for what was probably going to be the war to end all wars between the Costilla and Los Zetas cartels. With all the media attention her federal case was receiving, she couldn't afford being seen near a cartel warzone.

As she was walking down the jet's stairs next to Blake, she leaned toward him and said, "Can you make me a promise?"

"Yeah, what kind of promise?"

"Don't look at me like I'm crazy after today, okay? Because I'm not. I just have to instill fear in these people to stay on top. Papi taught me that."

"Awwww shit," Blake said, knowing that something bad was about to happen.

And bad it was.

There were over a hundred Costilla Cartel and Mexican military soldiers waiting in the airport when they made it inside. The paparazzi were at the front doors with their cameras pointed right at Alexus.

She paused in front of them, squinting thoughtfully and smiling at the same time.

"Shoot them," she said.

Blake's mouth fell agape as he watched the soldiers raise their assault rifles and open fire on the camera crews, shooting them dead where they stood.

Mary screamed and wrapped her arms around Pedro.

Enrique showed a prideful smirk and put his prosthetic hand on Alexus's shoulder. "That a girl. Your old man would be proud," he said, shouting over the gunshots.

When the explosions of gunfire ceased, Alexus sauntered past the dead and bleeding bodies like they weren't even there. She ordered her men to destroy the cameras as she was led to an armored Humvee.

There were ten more camouflaged Humvees and more than two dozen tan-colored pickup trucks with .50-caliber machine guns mounted on the roofs, all lined up perfectly on the road leading away from the airport.

Blake got in next to Alexus and slammed the door shut. Enrique took to the passenger seat next to his nephew Sergio, while Pedro and Mary got in another Humvee.

"This is it," Enrique said, turning in his seat to address Alexus. "Gamuza's in our line of fire. Last we checked he was still there in his room. We'll have to be quick. No mistakes, no slip ups."

"When did you last check?" Alexus asked as she strapped on a bulletproof vest.

"Right before we got on the plane."

"Well, check again. Then check again. Keep checking all the way up until we've got that son of a bitch. He's not getting away this time. I'm here to avenge my grandfather's death, and I'll be damned if I leave Juarez without that coward's head on a stick."

Enrique got on the phone as Sergio pulled off behind the other Humvees.

Blake put a hand on the back of Alexus's neck and began to massage it. "You good, baby?" he asked.

"I'm fine. Put your vest on. Don't worry about me. We're gonna get this motherfucker today, you can believe that if you don't believe anything else."

"Did you really need to kill all those reporters?"

"Shut up, Blake. This is no time to sympathize. Screw them. They shouldn't have come looking for me with cameras. I'm a fucking cartel boss, not a celebrity. They got the story they came looking for."

"That's that Papi in you." Shaking his head, Blake strapped on a vest.

"You're right about that," Alexus said. Her eyes were fixed on the dusty road they were zooming down. Her heart was pounding. She wondered what she'd do when she finally came face to face with her family's worst enemy. "Gamuza's gonna get it a lot worse than those paparazzi just got it. I know that much. He'll regret the day he set foot in my grandparents' home."

Alexus's plans seemed airtight. Gamuza's death was inevitable. Today was the day he'd meet his maker.

They made it to the location just minutes later.

A shootout between The Zeta and Costilla cartels was already under way.

Blake and Alexus watched from their windows as it all took place. Within seconds their sight was blurred by gun smoke and fiery explosions. People were running in every direction as they attempted to flee from the grim reaper. Alexus saw a number of Zetas emerge from the building with their guns blazing, only to be gunned down by the .50-caliber machine guns.

"This is what happens to those who cross me," Alexus murmured.

"Huh?" Blake hadn't heard her.

"I said, this is what happens to those who cross me," she said, louder this time. "I'm Alexus Costilla. Some day, they're all going to understand exactly what that means."

Her men were now entering the building. Four helicopters flying high above them were gunning at the Zeta snipers on top of the building.

The gunfire went on for what seemed like an hour. Blake checked his vest to make sure it was properly secured to his torso. Alexus couldn't keep her eyes off the action. It was like being on the set of an Expendables movie. There were grenades being thrown, rockets being fired, guns of every caliber banging and booming and clapping.

And then it settled down to just a couple of shots every few seconds or so.

Enrique got word that the coast was clear. He got out and opened Alexus's door. Blake followed her out of the Humvee, holding the gold-plated AK-47 he'd brought from the Matamoros mansion.

They stepped on bloody clumps of flesh and gun shells as they sprinted to the building, surrounded by a phalanx of armed soldiers.

Alexus held her breath as they entered the building. It had a foul odor to it that was too much for her to take in.

She kept a hand on Enrique's shoulder as he led her down a flight of filthy stairs to a basement that was lit only by a small television and the flashlights her men carried.

Most of the flashlights were being aimed at one spot at the rear of the basement. She walked to it, expecting to find Gamuza.

Instead what she found was a large hole that had been hidden beneath a rug. It led to a well-lit underground tunnel.

"What the fuck are you all waiting on?!" She shouted in Spanish. "Get down there!"

She stood back and watched as soldier after soldier disappeared down the hole.

Then she took one of the flashlights and flashed it around the basement walls, and what she saw was an even bigger shocker than the escape tunnel.

Blake muttered, "What the fuck? Are you serious?"

Taped up on the concrete walls were posters of Bulletface the rapper.

Enrique chuckled once. "You've got another fan, I see," he said, unable to hold back the laughter.

On the small television, a Bulletface video featuring Lil Boosie was playing at full volume.

Chapter 27

Rita was in the courtyard giving the kids swimming lessons in the Olympic-size swimming pool when Alexus returned to the mansion with Blake by her side.

Dr. Melonie Farr was seated at their usual table.

King and Vari waved at Alexus and Blake as they sat down with Dr. Farr.

"You are not going to believe what just happened," Alexus started.

"There is absolutely nothing you can say to surprise me anymore," Farr said, shaking her head at what was to come.

Alexus told her what they'd found in Gamuza's basement as she poured herself a shot of tequila. Melz found it hilarious; Blake didn't.

"You're famous even in Mexico, Blake." Melonie was all smiles. "That's a good thing, you know. A lot of artists would kill to have their music being played by a Mexican cartel boss."

"Yeah, you're official now," Alexus added jokingly.

"Fuck y'all." Blake turned and headed into the mansion.

"Okay, famous man!" Alexus shouted after him. "Love you!"

"Alexus, you have serious issues." Dr. Farr shook her head. "So, you actually found the place where Gamuza was living? Wow. You could have turned that information over to the FBI. They've got a five-million-dollar award for his arrest."

"You must have taken ten shots already, huh?" Alexus asked. "Because if you think I'd ever turn anybody in you must be drunk."

"You're right. Excuse me. I'm used to dealing with people who don't traffic thousands of kilos into the country every month."

Just then, Pedro and Mary came walking into the courtyard. Mary had a whole bottle of Ciroc vodka in hand. She plopped down next to Alexus, looked at Melz, and said, "From now on, if I'm here and you're here, and these nutcases wanna go out and shoot up half of Mexico, I'm staying here with you. I am absolutely finished with Pedro if he takes me on one more crazy ass cartel trip. That shit is not normal, it's not fun, I didn't grow up like that, and I don't like it. Not one bit."

Pedro tried to give Mary a kiss on the cheek and ended up kissing the palm of her hand instead. He chuckled and excused himself into the mansion.

"So," Melonie asked Alexus, "what's going on with Blake's girlfriends? Did he leave them for you? Are you two officially back together? Tell me something. You know I went to school to be nosy."

"He claims he's done with them. I don't know. We'll see. You know how his ass can be when it comes to hoes and groupies." Alexus gave Melonie's drink a second glance. "What are you doing drinking? I thought you said you only drank on special occasions?"

"It is a special occasion."

Alexus looked around the courtyard, as if Dr. Farr's special occasion would reveal itself.

Finally, she asked, "What's the occasion?"

"You'll need to talk to Britney to find that out."

"Oh, Lord." Alexus dug her iPhone out of her bag and dialed Britney's number. She put it on speaker so the girls could hear.

Britney didn't waste any time delivering the news.

"Guess what, Alexus. You are not going to believe this."

"What?"

"Your charges are dropped! The lead prosecutor has dropped all but one of your charges due to lack of evidence. Flako was their only real source of information. With him dead, they have nothing. You're off the hook."

A sudden burst of energy sprang Alexus out of the chair she was sitting in and knocked it over backward. She leapt into the air once, twice, three times, then ran and dove headfirst into the swimming pool. When her head popped up out of the water, everyone was laughing joyfully.

"It's funny," Rita said. "When we got the news, Melz said you'd jump headfirst into this pool. Turns out she was right."

Alexus couldn't believe her ears. It felt like a huge weight had just been lifted from her shoulders. She was free of the federal indictments! The only thing she could think of that would make her day any better was if she somehow managed to catch Gamuza and avenge her grandfather's death.

The celebrations began immediately. Drinks and food for everyone, liquor and good weed for the grownups. Alexus bathed and changed into yet another fabulous gown, though this time she went back to her normal all-white attire. She put on one of the diamond necklaces and two of the diamond rings Blake had gotten her for her birthday, along with a pair of custom-made Louboutin heels that were covered in white diamonds and worth $1 million.

The one charge that she was still being prosecuted for was a felony drug possession for the eight pounds of marijuana and nine ounces of cocaine that had been found during the raid on the Matamoros mansion. Britney explained that the charge wouldn't stick. They'd find someone to take the charge for her. Half the mansion staff had already agreed to take the charge for a few hundred grand. Alexus would pay whoever took the blame far more than that, just to keep her record clear of felonies. It was a win-win situation for her.

The celebration was held in the mansion's ballroom. A bunch of Alexus's celebrity friends flew in for the festivities, knowing that there would be tons of cash flowing around for everyone invited, and Britney didn't miss a single millionaire when she sent out the invites.

When the party kicked off, Alexus found herself traversing the white marble floor shaking hands and hugging. Blake settled into a corner with Lil Wayne, Jay Z, and Nas, and Alexus kept glancing in their direction, wondering what kind of astounding music they were discussing.

She had seven Bugatti giveaways scheduled for the winners of a game of Heads up. Ten runner-ups would receive $1 million each and another $1 million donated to a charity of their choice.

Everyone could not wait to play.

Just before the game began, Enrique asked to have a word with her. She excused herself from a conversation she'd been having with Melz, Britney, Rita, Taraji and Mariah Carey surrounding the next season of Empire and followed Enrique out into the hall.

"Jesus, Enrique, this couldn't wait?" Alexus complained, raising her crystal stem glass of champagne to her lips.

"I've got an idea." Enrique glanced over his shoulder to make certain that no one was close enough to listen. When he turned back to Alexus he spoke in a whisper. "We can get Gamuza. I believe I know a way."

"Well?" She threw up a hand. "Out with it."

"Get Blake to perform here in Mexico. Make it a big event, promote it on television and radio all over the country. If Gamuza's as into Bulletface as those basement walls suggested, he might show up."

"That's the most ridiculous thing I've heard from you, Enrique."

"No...just listen." He ran his fingers through his short crop of raven black hair. "I think it'll work. As farfetched as it may sound, I think it'll get him. There will be too many people. He'll bite on that. I guarantee it."

"I'll think on it." Alexus turned and headed back into the ballroom, already trying to refocus on the Empire conversation but unable to shake off Enrique's idea. Maybe she could get Gamuza that way. She hadn't considered it until now.

She made it back to the group only to be pulled aside again, this time by Britney, who donned an expensive snow-white gown similar to the one Alexus was wearing. It was an all-white affair, and every woman here had come out in their very best white dresses and gowns. Even King and Vari, who'd been allowed a half hour with the adults before being ushered off to bed, had worn white.

"What is it?" Alexus said.

Britney had her iPhone in hand. "I, uh...just got a call from your sister. She claims one of your guys almost shot her coming after two of her friends. The two friends are Nona and Bubbles."

"Since when did they become her friends?"

"I haven't the slightest idea, but it's what she said."

"Yeah?" Alexus's brows furrowed. She had her own iPhone in hand, but she'd deleted her sister's number when she was told that Mercedes no longer wanted anything to do with her. "Text me her number. I'll call her after we're done here. Tell Enrique to call off the hits on Bubbles and Nona until further notice. But I want that bitch in Atlanta dead."

"All the news channels say she's been taken into custody for the time being. Witness protection, more than likely."

"I don't care. Find her. Blake can't cheat on me if there's no one to cheat with."

Alexus put on a forced smile and finally rejoined the conversation.

King Rio

Chapter 28

"I recorded this one last week. Put y'all in it at the end. You and Wayne. It go somethin' like this," Blake said, and sailed into "Reminiscing", one of his latest recordings.

"I remember nights, I didn't remember fights
I didn't remember all the guap I blew, them was the nights.
All my guys had the white, and we always ride with the pipes
'Cause niggas like slidin' to strike, better know where you ridin' at night
From the Chi to my home, that's MC to the G
My Gary niggas was never scary, on their P's with the heat.
I slung pebbles to fiends, eighths and nines to the trappers
We was all 'bout the money, diss us we turnt into clappers.
I was rollin' up loud blunts and burnin' em backwards
Was known to be wild, bruh, I was burnin' the actors
Now I'm rich as a bitch, I look back and think of the times
When I had to drink out the sink, for soda I didn't have a dime.
I had money and hoes, hoodrats now they thots
I had boxes of ammo, for my choppas and Glocks
Now I invest in stocks, invest in land and vacant lots
Came a long way from standin' in vacant lots wit K's and rocks.
Got all my family straight, eatin' bigger dinner plates
Winners circle, play where winners play now, and my business straight.
Most these niggas fake, listen let me demonstrate
Ask to see his PSI, Presentence Investigation
I bet he'll turn his back and laugh and leave if he's a rat
I never gave a statement, ask the state to check the fact
That's why when I speak it's real, the very best of rap
And now I rap with Hove and Wayne, the very best of rap...'

Blake wasn't sure if the rap gods would like the song but his uncertainty quickly changed when Wayne and Jay said they had to get on the track. Nas wanted in, too.

Of course Blake agreed to send them the beat first thing tomorrow. These were the guys he'd grown up listening to. He had several collaborations with each of them, and all the songs were classics that had made them all a few million dollars richer.

Reluctantly, Blake ventured off to meet and greet other guests, while his fellow rap kings went to their women.

He paused to talk to Ice Cube and Dr. Dre about the upcoming release of Straight Outta Compton the movie. Then it was Beyoncé he was speaking to concerning a collaboration. Kendrick Lamar, The Game (the only guest to break the all-white dress code by wearing all red), and Young Jeezy also expressed interest in possible collaborations for the summer.

By the time Blake made it to Alexus, the Heads Up game was well underway. Mostly everyone was seated in fancy white chairs. Alexus and Britney were talking with Ellen Degeneres, the daytime talk show host who'd invented Heads Up.

He pulled Alexus aside. "Baby, you are so beautiful tonight," he said, admiring her shape in the curve-hugging Chanel gown.

"You don't look too bad yourself." She pecked her lips against his. "Who would've thought things would turn out like they have? I mean, I'm free of all those charges, and your biggest fan is my biggest enemy."

"Ha ha. Very fuckin' funny." Blake feigned a smile.

"Enrique thinks you should do a show in Mexico to reel in Gamuza. What do you think?"

"I think Enrique should stop thinking."

"Don't be so close-minded. It could work."

"Sluuurp."

"Slurp? What the hell's that supposed to mean?"

"Means you can suck my dick if you think I'm gon' do some dumb shit like that."

Alexus scoffed at the meaning. "You black fucker." She punched his shoulder. "Slurp yourself, that's what you can do."

"Don't say no gay ass shit like that to me. Fuck wrong with you." He laughed. This time, he leaned forward and gave her a kiss. "I'm staying here with you now, baby. Just us and the kids. And Junior whenever his momma let me get him."

"You sure about that?"

"Yeah, muhfucka." Another laugh. Alexus snickered. "I ain't stayin' if you gon' keep denying me the pussy, though. You got me fucked up with that shit."

"Keep your dick out of those bitches and we have a deal."

"Bet." He reached out to shake on it.

"And you'll take a test first thing tomorrow to make sure there aren't any diseases running through your nasty ass blood."

"Damn, you think I'm burnin'?"

"You tell me."

Blake shook his head. "Bet." His hand was still extended.

Alexus shook it, smirking widely.

It ended up being a joyous time for all. Solange Knowles, Ice Cube, and Nas were among the Bugatti winners. Promises and plans were made as everyone got ready to leave. Pictures were taken, many of which would later debut on Instagram pages with a million or more likes in less than an hour.

Blake stood outside the front door next to Alexus and waved goodbye to the guests with her.

"Well," she said, "that was something, wasn't it?"

"I feel like I'm married to Oprah Winfrey," Blake replied sourly.

She gave his shoulder a second punch, and he retaliated with a well-placed slap to her ass as she turned around.

"Ouch. You jerk," she said, rubbing her plentiful bottom.

"You gon' be saying more than ouch when I get off in you."

"Not tonight. Test first, remember?"

Alexus laughed merrily, knowing that her denying sex to Blake was eating him up.

When they made it to the bedroom, she got a chance to see just how much it was bugging him.

133

After showering, he took an extra blanket to the sofa at the foot of their bed and fell asleep there.

Chapter 29

"Hello, is this Barbie?"

"Who is this? I hope you know that I'm changing my number on you psychotic—"

"Wait, wait, wait. This is Porsche Clark. Yes, I'm related to Mercedes Costilla, but trust me, we have nothing to do with what's going on with you. We're keeping our distance from those lunatics just like you are. Where are you? Can we meet?"

No answer came, and when Porsche looked at the screen of her smartphone she saw that she'd been hung up on.

"That bitch hung up on me," she said in a murmur of disbelief.

The four women in the room with her — Mercedes, Sasha, Bubbles, and Nona — all stared at her.

They were in the living room of Sasha and Porsche's lavish new condo in Oak Park. They'd gotten the place together after robbing Porsche's ex-boyfriend of his cash and drugs when he busted her head a few weeks ago. It was the kind of home that Porsche had always wanted.

She planned to let Nona and Bubbles stay here until someone got ahold of Alexus and settled the beef.

"She's dumb as fuck," Mercedes said, talking about Barbie. "I wanted to help the bitch."

"Fuck that bitch." Porsche sat down on the love seat with Sasha, shaking her head. There was a bag of Skittles on the coffee table; she ripped it open and dumped some in her mouth. "Let the bitch get killed." She looked at Bubbles and Nona. "Y'all will be good here. Nobody knows where we live. You're the first people we've even brought here. There's food in the pantry and refrigerator, and I'll go out and get whatever y'all need from the store every day."

Nona planted her face in her palms and sighed. Bubbles rubbed her back.

"This shit with Alexus is getting out of control," Mercedes said, getting up. She began pacing a tight circle next to the coffee table. "Technically, I'm supposed to be second in line for the

Costilla Cartel crown. I don't want it, but still...she's acting like I'm not even a factor because I'm done fucking with her. The bitch really got me fucked up."

Mercedes went to the living room windows and fingered down the blinds. She looked out and saw only passing traffic and pedestrians. She thought back to when she'd first learned that she was related to the famous billionaire Alexus Costilla. She'd been in a financial slump, recently fired from White Castle, unable to even purchase her deceased mother, Whitney Clark, a gravestone. She had happened upon some papers documenting her birth parents while packing up and going through her mother's things.

The rest was history. Ever since she met Alexus, life had been grand financially. If there was one thing the Costilla family had in abundance it was money. Billions upon billions of dollars in drug money that had been accumulated over the past century was now easily accessible to Mercedes. She'd gotten close to $50 million out of her sister before their split, and it had her feeling like a real boss.

She poured shots of Ciroc for everyone. They swallowed the burning beverage and went for seconds.

There were four 9-millimeter Ruger handguns with 30-round extended clips and green laser sighting on the table. Mercedes had eight men and four women posted on the corners outside for security, their guns stashed in bushes and underneath their Escalades.

She'd never been to war, but she and her crew were ready for whatever came their way.

"You fucked me up when you blew that nigga's head off," Porsche said. "I was just getting out the car to see what was going on."

"I'm fed up with Alexus and that damn cartel." Mercedes was pacing again. "She thinks she runs the whole fucking world, and that's not the case. This is Chicago. This is my city. I'm not taking that shit anymore. From now on I'm on her ass. We're gonna take over this city and run shit so smoothly that she won't even be able to visit without our permission."

"That's what the fuck I'm talking about, big sis!" Porsche got to her feet. "You know I can't stand them niggas no damn way.

Wish I would've shot Blake's hoe ass instead of giving him some pussy."

"Sit the fuck down. Yo' triflin' ass shouldn't have drugged that man," Mercedes said.

Porsche sucked her teeth and sat down. "I'm just saying. Just because they're rich don't mean shit. We're rich now, too. I can pay a nigga to get at them the same way they can pay a nigga to get at us."

Just then, the microwave beeped, signaling that Porsche's Salisbury steak TV dinner was done. She went and got it, along with a Pepsi, and offered none to either of the girls as she sat back down to eat.

Mercedes dialed her sister's lawyer again, knowing that Britney Bostic was never far away from Alexus.

There was no answer.

It was a quarter past midnight.

She redialed the lawyer's number, got no answer, and then dialed another number.

The man was named Isaiah Scott — Mercedes knew this from their days at Dvorak High School — but he went by Cup, or Red D.

"Hey, I need a favor from you," Mercedes said. She stopped pacing and looked at Porsche. "Remember when my sister told you about Blake and Alexus plotting on you over that time when Savaria was kidnapped?"

She heard Cup exhale through the phone.

"What's up now?" he asked.

"They're still fuckin' plottin', that's what! Man, do you wanna die or something? Because we've been giving you all the info you need to handle this nigga."

"I don't believe that shit, either. I know Blake knows who kidnapped his daughter. So what? I'm a boss, he's a boss. We're making millions together. I think your sister was lying, anyway."

Mercedes felt her lower jaw drop. She shook her head at Porsche. Her younger sister couldn't seem to do anything right. Porsche's only job had been to convince Cup to go against Blake, and she couldn't even do that.

"Well," Mercedes said, "you don't have to take my word for it, or my sister's, but I'm telling you the nigga's on one with you for real, and I don't wanna see you go out like Chinx Drugz just went out in New York. You know Blake's guys have machine guns. They're worse than Lil Reese when it comes to that gunplay shit. Wake up, Cup. Wake up before it's too late."

Cup paused; then, "What the fuck do you expect me to do? You know how rich I've gotten off him and Alexus?"

"Fuck him and Alexus! You've known me since I was a little ass kid. You've hardly known them for two or three years."

"And? What's your point?"

"My point is a good one. You know, if Alexus gets put out of commission, I'll be able to run that business of hers. You know the one I'm talking about. I'd be in charge when she's gone."

"She ain't going nowhere. Didn't you see the news? They just dropped all those charges. She'll be in play for a long while."

Mercedes crossed the room to the window and peeked out the blinds. She could see a couple of members of her team standing under the streetlights and sitting in their SUVs on one corner, but she'd have to step outside to see the rest of them.

"Look, I gotta go," Cup said. "Hit me tomorrow or somethin'."

"Think about what I said, Cup. I can run shit way better than that stupid ass sister of mine. I'm a big city girl. I'm from right here on the west side of Chicago just like you. That bitch is from some small town in Texas. I'm telling you, I can do it. Just promise that you'll ride with me when it comes to me taking over."

"You know I'm with you. Hit me tomorrow." Cup ended the call abruptly.

An overwhelming feeling of frustration filled Mercedes at that moment. She stood there at the window, thinking of a way to climb to the top of the streets with her team. She had the money to do it, but what she lacked was the connections.

Then an idea struck her. It clicked on in her head like one of those lightbulbs in the cartoons.

She dialed a final number and watched as Marko, one of her guys who was leaning against an Escalade, raised his phone to his ear.

"Lil bro, I need y'all to go to the strip club on 16th and Trumbull," she said, turning to smile at her sister. "Drive by and shout out "MBM gang", then shoot up the club. Do the same thing to The Visionary Lounge on the corner of Laramie and Chicago Avenue. Use a different car for the shootings. And call me when it's done."

King Rio

Chapter 30

Even in the deep sleep that she was in, Alexus felt movement over her face. Too sleepy to open her eyes, she rolled over onto her left side.

She heard a grunt.

Then her face was being splattered with a heavy liquid.

Her eyes popped open.

Blake was standing over her grinning, jerking his dick as it gushed semen all over her face.

He stepped back as she leapt up out of bed, furious.

"Bitch! I know you didn't just cum on my face!" she yelled.

She rushed him, and he took off running into his walk-in closet and slammed the door shut before she could reach him.

She pounded on the door. "I fucking hate you! You nasty bastard!"

"Should've gave me some pussy," he said, laughing.

"I'm fucking you up for this nasty shit. You better believe that."

She stormed off to the bathroom and washed her face in the sink. Blake rushed into the shower as she was drying her face with a bath towel.

"I can't stand your stupid ass. You dumb bitch." She slapped the glass shower door and then went and flushed the toilet, hoping the shower water would turn hot and burn him, but he quickly jumped away from the shower head.

"Should've gave me some pussy," he repeated. "Stop treatin' me like a muhfuckin lame. I bet you didn't deny that nigga T-Walk no pussy when you was fuckin' him. Treat me the same way, then."

Alexus scowled at him through the glass shower door, gritting her teeth in utter disgust. She had the mind to go and get her .50-caliber Desert Eagle and blast through the glass just to show him how seriously mad she was.

"I hope you know this isn't over. I'm getting you back for that. I mean good, too. Really good. Black bastard."

"Love you, too, baby." She saw his shiny gold teeth through the fogged up glass as he grinned, covering himself in curds of Dove soap.

A number of mean thoughts ran through Alexus's head. She considered bleaching hid clothes as payback, or breaking his two iPhones.

The second notion brought a conspiratorial smirk to her pretty face, but now that her anger was waning she decided to just join him in the shower.

She'd get him back later.

His grin widened as she stripped and removed her bandages. As she slid open the door and got in, his cocky grin turned to a concerned frown. He didn't like seeing her with stitches and staples.

"My bad, baby," he said as he started washing her back.

"Don't talk to me. Asshole."

"I said I'm sorry."

"Fuck you, Blake."

Alexus was thinking over Enrique's plan to catch Gamuza. In her opinion, Blake was being inconsiderate. If the shoe was on the other foot, Alexus wouldn't have hesitated to help him.

"You should rethink your position on the Gamuza idea," she said.

"Sluuurp."

"Slurp yourself. I'm serious. I want that motherfucker dead, Blake. His men came after my mom and our kids. We need to get him by any means necessary. Right now, you're the means."

"No the fuck I ain't. You better find another nigga. I'm not about to be bait for a cartel boss. I watched a documentary on the Zetas. Them muhfuckas chop off heads, too."

Alexus tried convincing Blake to go along with the plan for the rest of their shower, while they dried off and dressed, and even as they joined Rita and the kids for breakfast, but he vehemently opposed the idea and refused to go along with it. It was stupid, he said, not worth the risk.

"Daddy, what are y'all talking 'bout?" King Neal asked, dumping a spoonful of Cheerios in his mouth. "Who is Gamza?"

Alexus snickered. "Gamuza, baby. And he's nobody. Just a man your father's afraid of."

It was almost as if Blake's body had switched to slow-motion mode. His head turned slowly to Alexus. His eyes were no quicker. His eyebrows came together.

"Scared?" he said. "You can't name a nigga on earth I'm scared of. Period. Matter-fact, name one now."

"Gamuza."

"Aaaaan, wrong answer."

"I don't believe you," Alexus persisted. She was eating a bagel with cream cheese and grape jelly, the same as her mother. "If you're not afraid of him, prove it. Do a show in Mexico. Doesn't have to be in Juarez. It can be in Cancun at my resort, or in Mexico City. Your choice."

Rita dabbed a napkin across her thin lips. "Don't force him into this kind situation, Lexi. Gamuza's a dangerous man. Leave all that to Enrique and Pedro. They'll tend to it the way they're supposed to."

"Nah," Blake said, wiping his own mouth and slamming his napkin onto the table. "I'll do it. As long as I make a few million in the process, I'm all in. Fu— I mean, forget it. Just give me a date. I do shows for a living. We can do this twice, if that's what you want. Long's it make dollars it make sense to me."

Alexus rolled her eyes and leaned toward Vari. "He's lying, you know that?" She said it loud enough for everyone to hear.

"No, I'm not." Blake's tone became more and more resolute. "I'll do the show for $8 million. And I'm donating it to the mob."

"To who, the same Vice Lords who—" Alexus started, but she didn't finish. What she's intended to say was "...the same Vice Lords who kidnapped Vari and killed her mom?", but she couldn't say that. Not with Savaria at the table.

"Nah," Blake said, "to the Dub. To my Dub Life niggas, the niggas I started trappin' with. I'm giving it all to them. I don't need it. The hood need it more than I do."

"Fine. Schedule the concert. I'll pay for the promotion and I'll pay you the $8 million." Alexus smiled, feeling like she'd won the argument.

After breakfast Blake took the kids out to ride their horses at the stables, while Alexus met with Melonie in the doctor's upstairs office. It was where Alexus and Rita often went to vent their frustrations. Dr. Melonie Farr was being paid $2 million a month for her round-the-clock services to Rita and Alexus.

Alexus stretched out on the long white Italian leather sofa and interlaced her fingers over her chest, gazing up at the high ceiling's two gold and crystal chandeliers. She'd put on yet another white jogging suit to conceal her wounds. A gold necklace with a gold, diamond-encrusted pendant that read QUEEN hung from her neck. White diamond Chanel earrings dangled from her earlobes.

Like Britney Bostic, Dr. Farr had grown used to the all-white attire that Alexus demanded from all her employees. She wore a white Chanel dress with matching heels by the same designer.

"What's on your mind today?" Melonie began.

"Blake's trifling ass. Girl, let me tell you what he did this morning. Let me tell you how he woke me up."

"Oh, Jesus."

"He needs more than Jesus." Alexus grinded her teeth together. "The nigga jacked off and came on my face while I was sleeping."

Dr. Melonie Farr's mouth fell open. The ink pen she had in her hand hit her desk, and she eased back in her white leather swivel chair.

"I know," Alexus said.

Melonie laughed.

"It isn't funny," Alexus said.

"The hell it's not. He's your husband, so I can't really call him a perv. A prankster, maybe. Sweet Jesus, he's lost his mind."

"I wanted to kill him."

"I don't blame you."

"He's crazy."

"There are definitely some psychological issues." Melonie picked her pen back up and jotted something down on her writing pad.

"We went to Juarez to try and find that fucker who murdered my grandfather. He had a wall full of Bulletface posters, and the TV was on a video Blake has with Lil Boosie. I couldn't believe it."

"What do you think it means? Does he enjoy Blake's music or is he watching him for a different reason."

"That's what I'm worried about," Alexus said with a sigh. "That's what Enrique and I haven't told Blake. That seems to be the more plausible reason for his obsession with Blake, but we're keeping it from him. For now. Maybe I should have him do a concert here in Mexico. I talked him into it. He's ready for a show now. Says he'll do it for $8 million. I think it's worth it."

Melz tapped the ink pen on her chin. Her eyes squinted thoughtfully. She had barely a pinch of makeup on, just enough to perfect her beautiful visage. The tips of her fingernails were painted white and perfectly manicured. The tennis bracelet on her left wrist was full of 8-carat white diamonds and worth $750,000 alone. Everything from her desk to the windowsills in the office were trimmed in 24-karat gold. She was essentially the most sought after shrink Harvard had birthed, but her wise mind belonged solely to Alexus Costilla.

"I don't know if I should say this as a professional," Melonie said, "but woman to woman I think you're right in making him risk his life for you. After all he's put you through, he deserves to be put in a little danger. That man Gamuza wants you all dead, and he murdered your granddad. I can understand why you want him captured so badly. His men came close to getting your mom and the kids a few weeks ago. That's an enemy who must be dealt with heartlessly."

Alexus bit the inside of her bottom lip and thought for a long moment. She had the world in her hands and only a few enemies to dispose of. If it took using her adulterous husband to get one of those enemies then so be it. She didn't want Blake hurt, but he'd hurt her heart without caring how she'd feel, so risking harm to him felt like payback.

She twisted the big yellow diamond ring Blake had proposed to her with around her finger, biting her whole bottom lip now and breathing calmly.

"Britney says your maid Leonetta will take the blame for that drug possession," Melonie said. "Her son has throat cancer, and she needs the money to pay for his chemo treatments. I say you give her enough severance pay to take care of all of it."

"I'll give her whatever she needs."

"She'll be going to give her statement in court first thing this coming up Monday. I'd pay for her legal fees if I were you."

"I'll have Britney handle it." Alexus's expression twisted as she remembered the way Blake had awakened her. "Ugh, Blake is a real life sicko. I haven't got a clue why I married that black bastard."

"Because you're young and in love, Alexus." Dr. Farr dropped the ink pen on her desk. "It's as simple as that."

Chapter 31

King Neal had named his three-year-old black colt horse King James, because his best friend at school's name was James.

Savaria's white mare (which had one brown spot around her eye) was named Dora. She was named after the cartoon Vari had grown up watching.

Blake took them riding on the strongly built horses, enjoying their shouts of joy as they galloped along the dusty trail that encircled the stables.

Though Blake rarely ever posted family photos on Instagram, he snapped and uploaded a few during the horse rides, if only to preserve the memories of the fun times he'd shared with his children.

King wore himself out arguing with Vari and ended up getting a spank on the butt for calling her a "dumb nut".

"Respect your sister, King!" Blake chastised, shaking his son by the arm. "If you don't respect your sister, you're disrespecting me! You understand that?"

Blake delivered the rear-end slap, and it didn't draw a single tear from King. The little soldier apologized to Vari and kept it moving.

Following their time with the horses, Blake took them to the courtyard. They took off their shoes and sat with their bare feet in the water, Blake in between them to keep them from bickering back and forth the way they always did.

King put his big head on Blake's arm. Vari kicked her feet in the cool blue water.

"I'm glad Mommy's home," Vari said. "I wish my other mommy could be here with us. I remember her a little bit."

"Wanna watch the videos again?" Blake asked, referring to the cell phone videos that were still on Ashley Joy's Facebook page.

Vari shook her head no. "I don't like watching them a lot. I wish she wouldn't have went to God so early. She could have waited until I was at least ten."

Blake pulled Vari close for a warm embrace. He kissed her on the forehead. "Mommy is still here, baby. She's watching over us all the time. Don't ever forget that."

"I won't."

Vari wrapped her arms tight around Blake's waist and pressed the side of her head against his ribcage. He could tell by the strength of her hug that she was hurting, so he curled an arm around her and held her just as tightly.

For a long while they gazed at their reflections in the pool's rippling waters. It was early, 8:55 AM according to Blake's icy Hublot watch. He had on a pair of baggy white denim shirts with piles of hundred-dollar bills in each pocket and a white T-shirt with a bulletproof vest on underneath it and a shoulder-holster that held his gold-plated Desert Eagle strapped in its pocket under his left armpit. His usual bevy of necklaces was absent today. Instead he wore a single gold chain with a large gold Jesus piece.

Rita had dressed Vari in a cute little white sundress and braided her hair in zigzags. She'd dressed King in yet another of his white Gucci shirt-and-shorts sets — he had about a hundred of them. There was a scratch on the left side of his face where Vari had clawed him during one of their recent scuffles.

"Daddy," King asked suddenly, "are you staying here with us now or are you leaving again? Because I, I hate when you leave and be gone like that."

"I'm here to stay, King." This time the forehead kiss went to King. "I sent for your brother last night. He should be here in the next hour or so."

Last night before bed, Blake had called Tiffany Jenkins — his son Junior's mother — and told her he wanted Junior to come to the Matamoros mansion for the next couple of days to spend some time with his brother and sister. Tiffany told him that she'd been in bed with the flu, but that her friend Danielle would bring him. Blake promised to compensate them both for the trip, knowing that money was all they wanted at the end of the day, anyway.

Vari began telling him about a school teacher of hers named Mrs. D who had a colorful bird next to her desk that could talk like a person.

Blake was only half listening.

His mind drifted off to the Gamuza situation, and for the umpteenth time he reminded himself that the old guy had sent a team of gunmen after the very children that were now sitting on either side of him. The concert would be worth it. Catching up with the Zeta cartel boss and delivering some street justice was one thing that Blake truly wanted to do. He had never beheaded anyone, but he knew he'd do it to Gamuza in a heartbeat. Any man who threatened his family deserved whatever death they received, in Blake's honest opinion.

He wondered if Gamuza would really show up at the show, and why the old fuck was so interested in him in the first place. He could not imagine why the cartel boss would be so intrigued by him. Maybe Gamuza was more than an obsessed Bulletface fan, as his walls had made it seem.

Maybe it was a shrine for the man he wanted to kill.

When the idea struck Blake, he instinctively raised his head and glanced around the courtyard. He had no company other than the kids.

"Daddy," Vari asked, "can you make me a promise?"

He kissed her forehead again, more out of worry and the fear of losing her to the ongoing cartel wars than simple love.

"Yeah," he said. "What kind of promise?"

"I want you to promise me that you won't go to God early like my first momma did. I want you at all my graduations, games and stuff like that. I want to see you when you turn old like Grandma. I don't want you to ever go to God. I want you to stay here with me and...that brat on the other side of you."

King leaned forward to look at her. "Hey!" he said.

Blake laughed. "You both are way badder than I ever was."

"I'll send her to God," King threatened, raising a fist to show he meant business.

"You ain't gon' do nothing but get beat up like you always do," Vari said in the most unworried of tones.

This brought another laugh out of Blake. He realized then just how much he loved his children. He couldn't wait for Junior to come and join the fun.

They were just putting their shoes back on when Pedro's college-aged girlfriend came sauntering out to the pool in a red string bikini.

She was slender and stunningly attractive, with just the right amount of meat on her bones to give her the most eye-catching, perfect curves. Her hair was done in a short bob. Her ass jiggled like Jello as she walked.

King Neal ducked behind Blake's legs and peeked his head out to clandestinely spy on Mary as she climbed the ladder to the diving board.

"Awww," Savaria teased. "King's got a girl crush, King's got a girl crush."

"No I don't, you stupid head," King said, blushing.

"Yes, you do."

"No, I don't. Fart face."

Blake pulled King back around in front of him, and King immediately froze up and went dead silent.

"See!" Vari said in triumph. "Look at you. Can't even talk. Li'l scary self. Say something." She turned her attention to Mary, smiling deviously. "Hey, Mary! My brother over here has a crush on you!"

"Stupid fart face ugly girl!" King said, the words tumbling out of his mouth one after the other without a single breath in between.

Vari giggled and Blake laughed, shaking his head.

Mary waved at them. "I have a crush on him, too," she shouted back half a second before she dove in the water and swam away from Blake and the little ones.

King took off running across the patio and through the glass doors that led into the mansion's family room. He ran right past Enrique, who was walking out to smoke a cigar.

"Your other boy's here with his mother, I believe. Or maybe it's the friend of hers. I'm not sure. They look too much alike."

Tiff-Tiff and her friend Danielle did bear a striking resemblance to one another. Both were redbones with pie-shaped faces and nearly identical shapes.

"Alexus just finished up a session with Dr. Farr," Enrique continued. "Your appointment's in twenty minutes."

"My appointment?"

Blake gave Vari a soft push to the back of the head, signaling for her to head inside. She ran in after King, shouting "King's got a crush on Maaaaaryyyyy!" again and again until her she was too far away for Blake to hear.

Enrique lit his cigar. "Not with Dr. Farr. There's a doctor here to test you for sexually transmitted infections and diseases. Alexus paid him to come from way out in West Hollywood."

Blake briefly considered refusing to take the tests, but he didn't think he could go another night without fucking his wife. He'd missed her for far too long. Just tasting her the other night had left his dick throbbing with blood, swollen to complete erection. He'd awakened this morning to yet another brick-hard erection, and he'd gotten Alexus for leaving him in such a state of sexual frustration.

He left Enrique and Mary in the courtyard and went in to take the tests. The doctor — an older white gentleman with graying hair and thin framed glasses — had a chair set up in one of the mansion's extra bedrooms. He small-talked with Blake during the blood tests, asked how awesome was it to be a rap legend at such a young age, and how was it being married to the woman just about every man in the world lusted after. He asked a lot of questions. Blake answered them honestly. He said the rap and Hip Hop lifestyle was the best and that he wouldn't trade it for nothing in the world. He said Alexus was what most men called a dime piece but that none of her fans knew that she was just as regular and flawed as any other woman. He told the doctor about his other son, and the doctor was surprised that the news hadn't yet made its way to the front covers of the major magazines.

At the end of it all, Dr. Rush left with promises to contact Alexus with the test results within the next two hours. Blake didn't want to wait that long but he didn't have a choice. He went to the family room and played Grand Theft Auto 5 with King and Junior, while Vari sat down between Alexus's legs and got a couple of barrettes that had fell off the ends of her braids clamped back on.

Danielle — Tiffany Jenkins's friend who'd flown first class on the plane with Junior — sat on the sofa next to Alexus. The two young women were in a deep discussion concerning Lil Wayne's recent troubles with Birdman and Cash Money Records.

Blake thought that something wasn't right about Alexus's smile. It seemed false. She usually could not stand the presence of the girls he'd slept with, and their friends were treated with the same level of disdain.

This wasn't the case with Danielle. For some unknown reason, Alexus was being incredibly kind to Danielle, even going so far as to offer her own private jet to fly Danielle back to Atlanta whenever she felt like leaving.

Blake kept looking over at them and frowning as he played the game with his boys.

Then he got a phone call that threw off his entire mental balance.

It was a call from Cup, and the way the Chicago mobster spoke immediately upset Blake almost to the point of violence.

"Bitch ass nigga, that's what we on? Huh? You gon' send some niggas to shoot up my clubs, nigga!"

"Man, who the fuck you think you callin' a bitch ass nigga?" Blake dropped the PlayStation controller in King's lap and got to his feet, getting angrier and angrier by the second.

"I call it how I see it, nigga," Cup said. "I hope you know all that coming to Chicago shit is over. For you, Meach, Biggs— all you niggas. This my city! You shoot up my businesses, you don't get to do business. And if we see any one of you niggas in the area it's gunplay on sight. Fuck all this friendly shit."

Blake stomped out to the hallway, not wanting everyone to hear what he was about to say.

"Look, nigga, I ain't shot up nothin'! Watch your muhfuckin mouth. Stop accusing me of —"

"Fuck you, nigga. It's on sight," Cup said and hung up.

King Rio

Chapter 32

Alexus gave Blake a thoughtful look as he came back into the family room, looking angry all of a sudden and scowling at his iPhone. She could see his jaw muscles flexing, his nostrils flaring, his fist balling and unballing. He was ready to fuck somebody up, and Alexus wondered who that somebody was.

"Bae, what's wrong?" she asked.

"That nigga Cup. He claim I had some niggas shoot up his clubs in Chicago, when I ain't sent nobody at that nigga. The nigga trippin'. He gon' fuck around and get what he askin' for."

"I told you a long time ago we should get him taken care of. You're the one who wanted to deal with him on behalf of some guy you know who's from his neighborhood. Forget him. And watch your mouth in front of the kids."

"I'll murk that nigga," Blake muttered through clenched teeth. He was texting someone. "Telling Biggs to be on point about this shit. He said he was on his way to see his—"

Just then, Blake's phone rang again, and he stepped back out into the hallway.

Alexus turned to her newfound friend and smiled. "Tell me more about Tiffany. I'm surprised Blake's never mentioned her to me before."

"She's Vari's mom's cousin. Actually, she and I both are related to Ashley Joy, just on different sides of the family."

"So," Alexus said, "technically, Vari's brother is also her distant cousin, too?" She laughed. "Jerry, Jerry, Jerry...!"

Danielle fell over in laughter. Then Blake walked in and signaled for Alexus to join him in the hallway. The look on his face told her it was serious.

"Oh, shit," she muttered under her breath as she got up and went to him. "What did I do now?"

"You got muhfuckas goin' at Biggs's sister in Chicago?"

"I did at first. I called it off. Actually, Enrique's been giving the orders on that. I just told him I wanted those whores dead if you were gonna keep fucking them. You can't blame me for being mad

155

about who my husband's fucking. Like I said, though, I cancelled the orders. They're safe now."

"That's my nigga's sister. You can't just be putting hits on any and everybody." Blake put his hand on the wall over her head. He seemed furious. "Calm that crazy shit down, baby. I told you, I'm not fucking either one of them ever again. Just leave em alone."

"Okay. I said I did already."

He gritted his teeth.

Alexus got on her tippy toes and kissed him on the lips. "Love you."

"No the fuck you don't."

"I do. I love Blake, I love Bulletface, I love Bee Kay. Isn't that what your friends used to call you in the hood? Bee Kay?"

"Why are you being so friendly with Danielle?"

"Because she's being friendly with me. Jesus, is it against the law now for me to befriend people?"

"I don't trust that shit."

"I'm asking her all about this new baby mama of yours."

"You can ask me all that."

Alexus smiled and wrapped her arms around Blake's waist. She kissed his lips again. "Don't be so uptight, Blake. Everything's fine. I'm just glad to have you here with me again. I'm trying my best to keep you happy so you don't go out and make baby number four on me."

"Your ass is crazy, Alexus. Don't start doing that Aunt Jenny type of shit. I'm for real."

"I just got a text from the doctor." Her eyes lit up. "Guess who isn't burning like a dragon's pussy?"

Blake laughed. "Fuck you."

"Baby, you're clean! I'm so proud of you."

"I don't know what the fuck you're so surprised for. I told you I always wore condoms."

"Next time," Alexus said, her expression turning perilously serious, "I won't be so fucking nice about this type of shit."

"Won't be a next time."

"Better not be."

Alexus ducked under his arm and returned to the sofa with Danielle and Vari. They talked about girl things for the most part, hair, nails, and boys. Danielle had somehow managed to get an Atlanta Hawks player interested in her, and they'd been going out a lot lately. She claimed to have permanently cut all ties to her son's father, some no-good nigga named Lil Will, and she'd talked Tiff-Tiff into cutting off her ex J-Rock for the same reasons. Together she and Tiffany were living the life in Atlanta. The money Blake had paid for the child support payments he'd been missing all Junior's life was way more money than Danielle or Tiffany could have ever fathomed having at once. Though Tiffany had blown a lot of it on Junior, she'd also spent like crazy on wardrobes for herself and Danielle, which explained the diamonds and gold in Danielle's jewelry and the Birkin bag under her arm.

"This bag cost fourteen thousand dollars," Danielle was saying. "I know you're probably used to having bags like this, but I'm not. This is truly a first for me. I feel like if I go back to the hood I'm gon' get robbed or somethin'. Everybody's been asking me to come back but I'm like "Nah, bruh." I can't do it. I'm keeping my ass in the A where the real money's at. Ain't nothing in my old city but bullshit weed, bullshit niggas, and a lifetime of probation."

"You're always welcome to come here," Alexus said as Vari got up from the floor and sat beside her. "Let Tiffany know that I'm not mad at her about any of this, either. If anything I'm glad my son has a brother. He needs a brother. Him and Vari go back and forth at each other's throats all day long. Maybe she'll get some peace now."

"Lord knows I need it," Vari said, and Alexus and Danielle burst out laughing at the young girl's grownup way of talking.

The conversation went on for several more minutes before Alexus noticed that Blake hadn't returned from the hallway.

She got up and went searching for him, checking the courtyard, the garage, the bedrooms, and even the front driveway before she finally settled on calling him to ask where he was.

When he answered, she laughed. "You are not going to believe what just came out of your daughter's mouth."

"I wouldn't be surprised."

"Where are you?"

"In the vault. I needed some time to think. This the best place to think in this whole mansion."

"I'm on my way down there in a second," Alexus said.

She went to her mother's bedroom and peeked in.

Rita was napping.

"Ma!"

Rita's eyes cracked open. "What do you want, Alexus."

"You wanna watch the kids while I go down to the vault for a minute? Blake's going through some stuff. Think he may need somebody to talk to."

Rita groaned and turned over. "Give me ten more minutes and I'll be out there."

"Momma, you're being lazy. Your grandkids need you."

"Make that singular. You have one son, that means one grandson for me."

"Mean old lady. You know Vari thinks you're her granny, too."

A pillow came flying in Alexus's direction. She managed to shut the door just before it could hit her in the face.

When she turned around, she was standing face to face with Enrique.

He towered over her with an unlit cigar protruding from the corner of his mouth. His white Armani suit was runway-fresh.

Alexus took a step back to keep from straining her neck to look up at him.

"Creep," she said, planting a hand on her hip. "What do you want?"

"Why'd you kiss me?" he asked.

Alexus paused and smirked. "No reason," she said finally. "Was horny, I guess. Why? You didn't like it?"

"I might have liked it too much."

"Hmm."

"Yeah."

Alexus rolled her eyes. "Anything else?"

"We've gotten a venue approved for Blake's show in Mexico City. It's the Aztec Stadium. Just $10,000 to rent it out. Should I set it up for this weekend?"

"Yes. And tell Britney I want her to spend whatever she has to spend to make sure it's promoted in every Mexican household. I don't care if it costs $20 million. I wanna be certain that if Gamuza goes looking for anything about Bulletface, he'll find it within seconds."

"What's with the new girl in there?" Enrique said. "She your friend?"

"She's the best friend of Blake's other son's mom."

Enrique smiled around the cigar. "You aren't going to do what I think you're going to do, are you?"

Alexus beamed. "Of course not." She stepped around Enrique and headed back to the family room, hating that Enrique knew her so well.

King Rio

Chapter 33

The elevator in the foyer could take anyone three stories below ground to a bank-like vault full of cash if the person knew what they were doing.

Blake knew the trick.

All it took was for him to hold the down arrow for thirty seconds before getting on the elevator, and that's exactly what he'd done.

Now here he was, sitting on a large, cellophane-wrapped square of cash that amounted to a little over $500 million, holding an AK-47 on his lap and a Styrofoam cup of Lean in his other hand, inhaling from the blunt he had secured between his lips, gazing vacantly at the screens of the two smartphones on his lap, thinking back to when his life hadn't been lived so dangerously.

There were several rooms in "The Vault", including a glass-walled bedroom, a bathroom, a small kitchen, and a larger room with a blacked out Bugatti Veyron Super Sport in the corner by a garage-like door that opened into an underground tunnel that would lead the Bugatti out to a distant empty field if the need to escape ever came. Years ago when Blake had been on the run from the States, he'd spent a lot of time down here. He'd initially been overwhelmed by the huge blocks of cash, but now it was nothing to him.

His mind was on the Cup situation. Maybe it was finally time to end Cup's life. It was bad enough that he'd let Cup live this long after having had Vari kidnapped years prior. Blake didn't know if all the money Cup had accumulated was getting to the gang leader's head or what but it was past time to put an end to all the bickering.

It was sad, too. Blake had grown to like Cup and all he stood for. Cup was a legitimate millionaire and a low-key leader of one of Chicago's most known street gangs. He'd survived federal drug raids and indictments several times, always staying far away from hand to hand sales and off the phone with his workers.

"I wonder who shot up the clubs," Blake said thoughtfully to himself. "What made him think it was me?"

He decided to Facetime Meach and get his feedback on the issue.

"Somebody must have told him the shooters came from you, bruh," Meach said when he'd heard the whole story. "That shit don't even sound right. We been rockin' with the nigga for too long. He got somebody in his ear, bruh. That's my guess. Here go Biggs. Ask him."

Meach handed the phone to Biggs, and just as Blake was getting ready to give Biggs the same rundown of the story he'd given Meach, Biggs shook his head and said, "I don't give a fuck about Cup. What's up with Alexus sendin' killers at my sister's head? The fuck is that shit about?"

"I know, bruh. She was trippin'. I got her to call that shit off."

Biggs didn't stick around for any more talk. He quickly passed the phone back to Meach.

"We'll deal with Cup, bruh," Meach said. "We just landed in Chicago about forty-five minutes ago. I'll slide on Cup right after we pick up Nona. I guarantee you some bitch or nigga is in his ear telling him some faulty shit."

"That's what it is, then. Hit me back." Blake put the phones and the assault rifle down next to him and smoked his blunt in peace. He didn't want to call anyone else, nor did he wasn't too even see anyone else. Not unless they were his family or children. He was tired of the world and all the daily drama that came with it.

There was an electronic 'Ding' as the elevator made it to the vault, and he knew that it had to be Alexus.

Sure enough it was.

She'd brought Danielle with her, and Blake immediately wondered why. This was a secret room that hardly anyone knew about.

"Baby, are you alright?" Alexus asked as she sauntered over to him.

"I'm good," Blake said tersely.

Danielle's eyes were flicking every which way, awestruck by the vastness of the secret vault, and by the big blocks of brand-new Benjamin Franklins.

"This is some James Bond type shit right here," she said.

Blake leaned forward and whispered: "Why would you bring her down here?"

"Because."

"Because what?"

Alexus shrugged her shoulders and set her red leather Chanel shoulder bag down on a separate block of cash...which is when Blake noticed that she'd changed clothes.

She had on a dark red pair of Chanel sweatpants with a matching T-shirt and red five-inch Louboutin heels.

"The fuck you got on red for?" he asked, but Alexus ignored him.

Instead, she dug in her shoulder bag and came out with a big bottle of Hennessy and three shot glasses with Chanel's double-C logos on the sides.

Alexus often wore Chanel because of its double-C logo. She always said it really stood for Costilla Cartel.

"Let's get in a couple of shots to ease the stress." Alexus climbed up on the block of cash and helped pull Danielle up to sit next to her. "I don't wanna hear anything negative. Forget Cup, forget Gamuza, forget the judge and that filthy prosecutor. It's all about us."

"Fuck Cup and Gamuza," Blake agreed, taking the bottle of cognac from Alexus and removing the top for her.

He poured the shots and the three of them turned them up in unison. A tattoo on Danielle's forearm caught Blake's attention. It read "Lil Will" in black cursive letters.

He knew a Lil Will he'd met a long time ago in Harborside Projects in his hometown. The apartment buildings were gone now, replaced by the Blue Chip Casino, but he remembered Lil Will more than he remembered anyone else from the projects because Lil Will had stolen his bike, spraypainted it, and then rode it right past him as if he wouldn't notice that it was his stolen bike.

He and Will had fought in someone's front yard for a good five minutes about that bike. Blake had won and taken the bike home.

He asked Danielle if the tattoo was for Lil Will from Harborside and she said it was.

"That's my baby daddy," she said, her face all screwed up as she swallowed the shot and reached out for another.

Blake poured everyone seconds, and again they took them together.

"I'm done with this shit," he said, handing the bottle to Alexus. "I'm not about to be drinking this and sippin' my Lean at the same time."

Out of the blue, Alexus turned to Danielle and asked, "Have you ever had sex with a girl before? If not, would you do it for $10,000?"

Danielle cracked up laughing. "I'll have sex with ten bitches for ten thousand dollars. The fuck? What did you expect me to say, no?"

Blake and Alexus laughed with her, and Blake found himself wondering if Alexus was being serious or playing around.

He hoped she was serious.

One of his smartphones rang again. This time it was Tiffany calling.

He didn't want to answer it.

Not in front of Alexus.

Not even a week ago, he and Tiff had enjoyed themselves a night in front of the television off the very same liquor that Alexus was now filling her shot glass with, and the night had ended with him in bed with her. Since then she'd sent him several suggestive text messages and seductive pics of her in the skimpiest outfits she owned.

"Who's that?" Alexus asked as he hopped down to the steel floor.

"Nobody. Hold on," he said, and answered the call.

"I'm busy, Tiff. What is it?"

"Junior didn't bring his inhaler, so make sure you keep him from doing anything too strenuous unless you have an extra inhaler laying around somewhere."

"Damn, the lil nigga got asthma?"

"Bronchitis. It's basically the same thing. Just keep his ass sitting down."

"I'll send somebody out to get him an inhaler today."

"Good...so, what y'all doing now? Can we talk?"

"Not really."

"She's right there, isn't she?"

Blake chuckled. "Yeah."

"Make sure that bitch keeps my baby away from those Mexican cartel niggas. I ain't got time to be acting up and going to jail right now, tryin' to open up this hair salon out here soon."

"He'll be good here with me, a'ight? No worries. And like I said, I'll send for him an inhaler today."

"Okay." He heard her suck her teeth through the phone. "Call me sometime today, too. I wanna hear from my baby."

"Our baby," Blake corrected.

"Yeah, whatever. He was my baby before he was yours."

Blake rushed Tiff off the phone and sighed through his nose when she finally hung up.

He turned around to put his attention back on Alexus just as she was dragging her heavy, goldplated Desert Eagle pistol out of the shoulder bag.

Blake's eyes went wide.

Danielle had her shot glass turned up in the air.

"Baby, don't —" Blake started.

Then he flinched as Alexus put the gun's large barrel under Danielle's right ear and pulled the trigger.

The gunshot echoed fiercely throughout the stainless steel vault. The innards of Danielle's skull went to the ceiling as she fell off the big block of hundred-dollar bills. Her head hit the floor with a sickening thud.

Blake stared at his wife, his ears ringing so hard that he had to read her lips to understand what she was saying as she put the bulky gun back in her bag and poured herself another shot of cognac.

"I told you about fucking around on me. That's for everything you did while I was in that coma. Now, fuck around on me again and see what happens."

King Rio

Chapter 34
Two days later...

'Good evening, ladies and gentlemen. I'm Anderson Cooper, and we're live outside Alexus Costilla's home in Matamoros, Mexico, a town on the other side of the border from Brownsville, Texas.

'I'm sure you all remember when just a couple of years ago two of Alexus's close friends — Cereniti Stingley and Jantasia Olsen — who'd been visiting her at this very estate, went missing and have never been heard from again. An international search for the two young Harlem women yielded no real leads, and three hundred and forty days after they went missing U.S. District Attorney James Flanagan closed the case, believing them to be deceased.

'Well, it's happened again.

'Tiffany Jenkins, an Indiana woman who recently learned that rapper and Hip Hop mogul Blake "Bulletface" King fathered her now four-year-old son, admits to sending her son to visit his father here at this mansion earlier this week. She sent him with Danielle, the childhood friend of hers who has gone missing just like Jantasia Olsen and Cereniti Stingley. Alexus and Blake's family attorney claims the young woman left for the airport and promised to phone them when her flight landed safely in Atlanta, but the call never came...'

Blake was on the edge of his seat in his Gulfstream 650 private jet, his eyes bloodshot, an ounce of Kush and twenty blunts spread across the middle of the table in front of him. He was watching CNN on the 40-inch curved TV. Every couple of seconds or so he glanced out his window to try and see the camera crews from his vantage point on the runway, but he was too far away from them. All he saw was a bunch of lights.

His jet was parked behind Alexus's on the Matamoros mansion's private runway. Meach was across the table from him. They were both dressed in black T-shirts over black Balmain jeans and black and gold Louis Vuitton sneakers. A slew of gold and diamond necklaces bearing the MBM logo on the pendants encircled their necks.

The four others on the plane with them were music engineers and Blake's road manager.

Two days had passed since Danielle's murder.

In less than two and a half hours, the Bulletface concert at the Aztec Stadium in Mexico City was due to begin.

"This is the kind of shit that made me cheat on that crazy bitch," Blake said, shaking his head. "Do you know how many times we've been on CNN? This shit is ridiculous. I should go back to Bubbles and Nona."

"And get them killed like Danielle?" Meach said.

Blake shook his head and sipped some Lean. His iPhones were ringing off the hook, mostly from Tiffany and Danielle's people. They wanted to know what happened to Danielle. They wanted closure, and that was something Blake couldn't give them, so there was no need in answering their calls.

Although he'd never tell a soul, he knew that the closure they were after was cut up in five pieces and buried in a shallow grave somewhere on the outskirts of Matamoros.

"Bruh, you gotta change your phone numbers." Meach sipped from his Styrofoam cups. He too was focused on the television.

"Let em keep calling. I don't care." Blake dropped his head back against the headrest and shut his eyes. "I'm tired of this lifestyle, bruh. Getting married to Alexus might be the absolute worst decision I've ever made."

"You're a better man than me," Meach said. "Ain't no way in hell I could go through all the shit you go through with Alexus. You lost Moms and Pops. We lost Young D, Lil Mike, Yellowboy, and Pat. Seems like we was safer before you met Alexus than we is now. She still holdin' out on the pussy?"

"I ain't even tried since she whacked Danielle. I really don't even want to. I wanna fuck Bubbles. Or Nona. Barbie done disappeared on me. I think she's in some kind of witness protection program now. Shit's crazy."

"You might just need to get the fuck away from wifey for a minute. Give yourself some time to think. After this show in Mexico, just dip off somewhere by yourself and figure out exactly what it is you wanna do. It'll come to you."

Meach's suggestion wasn't new to Blake. He'd thought of vanishing on Alexus every hour on the hour since she killed Danielle. But there was a special place in his heart for Bubbles and Nona, and Alexus had already threatened to have them killed if he left her again.

When their planes took off into the air moments later, he was thinking of a way to leave his wife while at the same time keeping his side chicks safe from the Costilla Cartel. It wouldn't be an easy task, he knew that much. Not with Alexus's ocean-deep pockets and ruthless team of loyal killers.

"It ain't good for you to keep being on the news like this, bruh," Meach said.

On the television, Anderson Cooper was bringing up all the people who'd gone missing or were killed because of their ties to Blake and Alexus.

The list was a long one.

"No shit," Blake said to Meach. "And now the crazy bitch got me on a suicide mission, going to Mexico City to perform in front of some muhfuckas who probably won't even understand what the fuck I'm sayin', just to try and catch the boss of the fuckin' Zeta cartel."

"Like I said, you're a better man than me. Only reason I'm even coming to this show with you is 'cause you my bro. If it wasn't for our history my ass would be as far away from here as possible."

Blake understood Meach perfectly. They'd been practically born and raised in the same households, went to all the same schools, and fucked a lot of the same neighborhood girls. They'd ran from police together and fought together. Everything.

For the rest of the flight they smoked blunts and discussed ways for Blake to end his relationship with Alexus...before he ended up being the next chopped up body the Costilla Cartel was responsible for.

King Rio

Chapter 35

"Blake's gonna leave you for good if you don't calm down with the jealousy," Enrique said.

Alexus rolled her pretty green eyes and said nothing. There was really nothing to say. Blake was lucky that her men had failed in their attempts to take out his side bitches. He'd slept with every whore under the sun while she'd been in the hospital, and in her opinion, he deserved some punishment for such bold acts of disloyalty.

She reclined her seat and took a deep breath. She had to focus. Her plan to finally catch the Zeta's asshole boss seemed to be working perfectly.

She'd gotten word that earlier in the day a group of alleged Zeta cartel militants had overran a small police station in Mexico City, killing fourteen officers and capturing eight more. Although Alexus didn't have a clue as to why Gamuza would want a bunch of police killed, the operation itself was solid proof that Gamuza had his sights set on Mexico City.

Enrique's warning meant little to her. He was only saying it because her men had located Barbie and were going to try kidnapping the bitch any minute now.

As bad as Alexus wanted to give up on her hatred for her husband's mistresses, she knew deep down that he would eventually go back to them, and that was a pill she had a hard time swallowing. She didn't know how she'd live if Blake ever left her for good, especially if it was for another woman. Her heart had been ripped apart when he'd dated Nona a few years ago, and even though it had been her fault for cheating on him with T-Walk, she still wanted Nona dead for fucking around with Blake.

To get her mind off the troubling thoughts, Alexus picked up her iPhone and went to Twitter to see what her favorite celebrities were up to.

She checked Taraji P. Henson's page and saw the usual loving retweets. A look at Oprah's page revealed a new reality show on the OWN Network. Erica Dixon was single again. Joseline Hernandez had just posted telling the fans that her Instagram page was hacked. Taylor Swift wished Kendrick Lamar was her best friend.

The simple things all the rest of Hollywood was going through made Alexus feel even worse instead of better. She was the wealthiest of them all, yet she was living life on the edge while everyone else seemed to be relaxing and enjoying themselves in the warm summer weather.

She left Twitter for Instagram and went searching for the pages that belonged to Bubbles and Nona.

Unsurprisingly, the pages had been deactivated. All that came up were pages with similar names.

The same thing happened when she went in search of Baddie Barbie's page. It too had been taken down.

Alexus snickered once and slapped her knee in amusement. "Scary ass hoes. Where'd they go?" She looked across the table at Enrique, then across the aisle at Pedro and Mary. "They're hiding from me. Where'd they go?"

"You're crazy," Mary said matter-of-factly. "I used to look up to you so much. You were like Beyoncé in my eyes. Not anymore, though. I see now that you're just another nutjob like your aunt Jennifer was."

"No," Alexus refuted, "I'm not crazy. Blake is the crazy one. I just know how to get even. There's a big difference between being crazy and getting even. Sometimes it takes one to do the other, you know what I mean?"

"No, I don't." Mary wouldn't look at Alexus.

"Well, maybe it's not meant for you to understand. But I know something that you will understand. I'm the queen around here, and the next time you call me crazy I can personally guarantee that something terrible will happen to you quicker than you can say 'crazy'. You got that?" Alexus didn't wait for a reply. "Good. Now sit over there and mind your fucking business if you don't have anything nice to say."

Mary's comments pissed Alexus off, and she was glad that Pedro's smart-mouthed little lady didn't have anything else to say.

She took a selfie of her scowling and uploaded it to Instagram with the caption: #WhenABitchGotYouFuckedUp

A flood of heart-eyed emojis appeared in the comment section within seconds. She read through the comments and was immediately drawn in to the love. She was up to 58.4 million followers now, and mostly all of them — the ones who commented, at least — seemed to love her unconditionally.

"My Instagram followers are the shit," Alexus said, smiling all of a sudden. "They love me more than Blake's selfish ass ever will. You know what? I might just leave that black fucker and find myself a football player or something. I might as well. Rappers are too slutty for my taste."

"You're full of you know what," Pedro said. "We all know it."

"Exactly," Enrique agreed.

Alexus gave the two men a middle finger to share and went to the photo she'd posted yesterday. It was a picture of Savaria sitting on her horse with the biggest smile on her face. There were 247,877 comments under the picture. Most were good, but there were some haters. Alexus never got how some people could come on social media and hurl insults at the most innocent of photos. Seeing it always made her grit her teeth and shake her head. There were numerous times when she'd went to the hater's pages in hopes of finding out who they were just so she could send her goons to pay them a visit, but every time she'd found that their pages were private.

This time was no different. She tapped on the names of four different internet bullies and found all of their pages to be private.

With her appetite for Instagram suddenly diminished, Alexus put the phone down and stared at Enrique.

"You look so strange dressed that way," he said.

Alexus had on red lipstick and fingernail polish to go along with her red Chanel dress. She'd had her hairstylist put a single streak of red down the leftside of her long black hair.

"I look like I'm supposed to look," she countered. "Every time I'm forced to deal with my cheating husband's mistresses, this is how I'll look."

"Yeah, but it still looks strange. We're so used to the white."

"Well, get used to it." Alexus sounded serious. "We're gonna be seeing a lot of red these coming days if he doesn't straighten up and act right. I'm done playing games."

Chapter 36

Mary's feelings were hurt.

She'd never been so totally pissed and horribly afraid in her life. She wanted to leap out of her seat and give Alexus a piece of her mind, but she knew from watching the news over the years that nothing good ever came to those who went against Alexus Costilla.

Still, though, Mary couldn't control her anger at being so rudely disrespected. Tears sprouted up in her eyes. She balled her hands into fists and got up, but instead of swinging at Alexus like she wanted to she went to the restroom.

Pedro was on her heels. He caught the door just as she was slamming it shut and stepped in behind her.

"I hate that bitch already," Mary said, leaning back on the sink as Pedro closed the door.

"I know you're upset—" he started, but she quickly cut him off.

"You're damned right I'm upset! Why didn't you say anything?"

"Because sometimes it's best to let a blind woman keep walking when she steps on your shoe."

Mary turned to him with the right side of her upper lip raised in a scowl. "I don't wanna hear your philosophical answers, okay? Plain and simple, I'm your woman. You should take up for your woman. It's what a man's supposed to do."

"Yeah, but she's the boss." Pedro unbuttoned his shirt; it was warm on the plane. He unzipped his fly and went to the toilet for a piss. "The thing is, Mary, I can't go against anything Alexus says or does. She's the boss of the cartel until the day she dies or goes to prison forever. Since it doesn't seem like she's going to prison any time soon, we all have to suffer through her emotional rollercoaster ride with her rap star hubby. I don't like it, Enrique doesn't like it, and none of our soldiers and workers like it, but there's nothing we can do about that."

"Who's next in line?" Mary asked, wiping her eyes with a tissue as Pedro flushed the toilet and washed his hands in the sink. "To run the cartel, I mean. Who will run it if Alexus dies?"

"It's supposed to be me, but the position will have to be offered to Mercedes first, since she's Alexus's only sibling. She'll probably turn it down, though. She's terrified of the cartel. She won't even talk to us now."

"Can't say that I blame her."

"Are you okay, Mary?" He lifted her chin in his hand and gave her a firm kiss on the lips. "Don't let her get to you. She's lovestruck and absolutely clueless as to what's really important to the cartel. All she thinks and cares about is Blake. There's nothing either of us can do to change that."

"We need to somehow get you to her spot," Mary said, as if it was the first time she'd thought of it.

"Don't be foolish."

"I'm not being foolish, Pedro. You know that girl doesn't have what it takes to run a fucking drug cartel. She's a 23-year-old kid from Brownsville, Texas. She hasn't gone to college, she hasn't tried to gain any more knowledge than the little bit she learned in high school, and now all she does is strut around in her expensive dresses and heels, letting her cheating husband drive her insane. You tell me, what kind of drug cartel boss is that? It certainly isn't one I'd want to be taking orders from."

"I know." Pedro couldn't argue with the truth.

"And what about this trip we're going on now? Are we really going to try and find the boss of another cartel? For what? To kill him?"

Again, Pedro could say nothing. Mary was right on all counts. Alexus was young, dumb, and crazy in love with a gangster who she'd made a rich man. There was no way to get Alexus off the deadly rampage she'd been on lately. She was a scorned married woman, Pedro reminded himself, a woman whose father had been murdered by her own husband. The Costilla family was the most dangerous family Pedro had ever known, and it pained him to be a part of it. He wanted to reign supreme, but his lovestruck little cousin Alexus was in the way.

"We have to do something," Mary said in her whiniest tone. "Be the man, the leader. Turn this thing into something good."

"There's nothing I can..." Pedro's voice trailed off into a stunned silence as Mary pinched the bottom of her black Valentino dress between her thumbs and forefingers and eased it up to her waist.

She was naked under the dress. Naked and clean-shaven.

Pedro hardly had time to take in the sight of her lower region before she pulled him to her for another, more passionate kiss.

He could not help it — he delved one finger inside her wet opening, then two.

She squirmed under his touch.

"Make me a queen, Pedro. A queen. You be the king. Don't be a fool for your cousin," Mary pleaded as her breathing hastened.

Pedro lost his train of thought as he dropped his pants and drawers and sank his love muscle as deeply into her as it could go.

She inhaled sharply.

Her sex was tight and warm. It squeezed his muscle and drew it in deeper. His mouth found hers, but instead of his normal, calculated kisses, he clumsily bumped and rubbed his lips on hers as he began to thrust.

She put one leg up on his shoulder; he kissed its ankle and kneaded its thigh in his hands, keeping an eye on her ecstatic expression as continued to slam his hips forward.

He glanced at his reflection in the mirror and instinctively smiled. He realized that he was finally getting what he'd been wanting for weeks now, and it felt even better than he'd imagined it would.

Mary tried to hold her silence but several involuntary yelps escaped her lips. Her mouth hung halfway open. She ended up having to slap a palm over her mouth to keep from yelling out.

The sudden urge to press a hand to Mary's throat overcame Pedro so he did it and didn't regret it. He pounded harder and harder. She yelped and moaned, holding on to her small, jiggling breasts.

Looking down at his rapidly pumping erection, Pedro noticed that his member was fully coated in Mary's creamy juices. Just seeing the wetness on him made him thrust harder.

Her hands went under his shirt and she dug her fingernails in his back as he leaned over her and started licking and kissing the side of her neck.

Suddenly, the doorknob shook.

"What the hell are you two doing in there?" Alexus said.

Mary's eyes went wide, and so did Pedro's, though he kept on thrusting as if Alexus hadn't said a word.

Chapter 37

Blake's private jet and the Boeing 787 that carried his and Alexus's vehicles were the first to land at Mexico City International Airport.

He and Meach packed up their Kush and Lean into the Louis Vuitton suitcases where their clothes, jewelry, and guns were stored.

"We should've brought the goons out here with us," Meach said as they sat and waited for their vehicles to arrive.

"You ain't lying," Blake agreed. "If there's one time we need every goon we got it's now."

Meach stood up and bent over to peer out his window. "Welcome to Mexico," he said thoughtfully. "If I run into Selena Gomez, just leave me here, bruh. For real."

Blake chuckled. "Shut the fuck up, nigga. That bitch ain't thinkin' about you. She on niggas like Justin Bieber, muhfuckas with that long bread. The fuck you gon' do with $21 million?"

$21 million was Meach's current net worth. Mocha and Will Scrill were right behind him with $19.5 million and $17.4 million. Biggs was in last place with $5 million.

"I can do enough," Meach argued. "Just because everybody ain't got a billion-plus like you don't mean these hoes ain't fuckin'. These bitches fuckin' broke niggas with two-dollar net worths. I know I can fuck whoever I want."

"What's up with Johnesha?"

"That's still wifey," Meach said with an untrusting grin.

"Yeah, right. I ain't seen you with her in forever." Blake took a large gulp of Lean

"I really want Malika," Meach admitted. "Ol' girl from the Kardashian show, played in the movie ATL with her twin sister. She bad, bruh. On Angelo."

Blake nodded. His mind wasn't with Meach but he was listening, or at least trying to.

What weighed heavier on Blake's mind was what he planned to do after the concert.

He picked up one of his smartphones and told his pilot to let him know when Alexus's flight landed.

Then he dialed Nona's number, taking a deep breath in through his nose and out through his mouth as it rang, gazing vacantly at the 7 carat yellow diamond on his pinky ring.

Gangster's intuition told him that she wouldn't answer, but he was wrong.

"If she's around you I don't wanna talk," Nona said as soon as she picked up.

"I wouldn't do you like that." Blake leaned back in his seat, suddenly relaxed and grinning his signature gleaming grin. "Where y'all at?"

"Why?"

"Damn, you think I'd set you up?"

He heard her sigh through the phone. She paused for a long moment.

"I'm scared, Blake. Your wife needs to be in a fucking mental institution."

"I know, I'm ending that shit today. I'm coming to get you and Bubbles and then flying to Barcelona, Spain for a few months. A vacation with just the three of us. I'm not telling a soul where we're at. We can put the room in somebody else's name, and if we like it enough I'll buy a vacation house there. I'm breaking my iPhones before we get there and using new ones from now on."

"What about your kids?"

Blake clenched his teeth and flared his nostrils, unzipping his duffle bag to get a grip on the handle of his Glock handgun. He found solace in its 50-round drum magazine, and the $250,000 in packets of hundreds that lay stacked under the perilous weapon was also comforting.

"I'll take my kids with me. That bitch Alexus needs help. I'm not staying around for that shit. She gon' make me do something to her before she can get me."

"You think she'd have you killed, too?"

Nona's intrusive question brought a look of uncertainty to Blake's face. He didn't know whether or not Alexus had it in her to order his murder, but the notion alone was unsettling.

"If it takes you that long to answer," Nona said, "you should be trying to stay away from her, too. And what's this shit with you and Cup being into it? I overheard Mercedes telling him something on the phone a few nights ago, and ever since then the streets have been saying he has money on your head if you come back to the Chicago. They say it has something to do with his clubs getting shot up."

Blake frowned and turned to Meach, who was busy rolling a cigarillo full of loud.

"What?" Meach mouthed silently.

Blake held up an index finger. "Mercedes talked to him right before that shit happened?" he asked Nona.

"Mm hmm. We were up taking shots and tripping over those people who came after us that day. She got on the phone with Cup, then she" —Nona gasped abruptly— "she called those niggas she had standing around outside, and when they came back they talked about a shooting! I don't know how I didn't connect the two. Damn. She had that shit set up so you and him would have beef. That dirty bitch."

Blake nodded as it all sank in. "Where you at?" he asked, going to his window as the pilot signaled that Alexus's plane was now coming in for landing.

"I'm in Chicago at Porsche's place. They've been gone since the other day, but they'll be back. She has two guys staying here with me. Bubbles went to New York. You know she has a house out there. I'd appreciate it if Alexus didn't find out where either of us are at."

"I'll be to pick you up tomorrow and we're gone, a'ight?" Blake snatched the blunt from Meach and sucked in smoke until his cheeks bulged. "Fuck all this shit."

"Okay...love you, Blake."

"Love you, too." He pressed end and stared at the phone before turning back to Meach. "Mercedes set up that shit between me and Cup."

"I knew somethin' was funny about that." Meach nodded his head tightly. "It didn't make sense."

"I'm about to be done fucking with all the Costillas. All of em snakes."

"Except Pedro. He kept everything a hun'ed," Meach reminded him.

Blake went silent as the jet's door was pushed open. He was standing in the same position when Alexus came sauntering up the stairs seconds later.

Her red dress and lipstick threw him off yet again. He was so used to her wearing all white every day.

She looked at him, then looked at the phone in his hand.

"Who were you taking to?" Alexus asked, smiling seductively as she walked to him.

Enrique followed in behind her.

"Fuck is you all in my business for?" Blake said, grinning. He draped an arm around her waist and pressed his lips to hers.

"You ready for this show?" She pulled back and studied his eyes.

"Of course I'm ready. I'm always ready." Blake's habit of grabbing and squeezing Alexus's ass was still alive and well. His hand roamed her buttocks.

She put her mouth next to his ear. "I'm mad, Blake. Pedro and Mary just fucked in the bathroom on my plane. I'm jealous about that. I want some of you." She looked around at Meach and the others. "Everyone out. Blake and I need a moment alone."

Chapter 38

She wanted to know who he'd been on the phone with more than she wanted to have sex with him but the phone call could wait...for now, at least.

The moment the others were off the plane, Alexus shoved Blake onto one of the white leather seats.

"Pull it out," she said.

"You're something else," he said, studying her just as closely as she was studying him.

He unbuckled his Louis Vuitton belt and reached in for his lengthy pole. Alexus stood over him and eyed his twelve-incher as he stroked it in his hand.

"I'm still afraid I might catch something from your trifling ass," she said, holding her hips.

"Don't start that shit again."

"I'm serious. I mean, you were fucking those bitches. No telling what kinds of diseases they got. It might be something that can't be detected through regular blood tests. You never know with these hoes nowadays."

She sat down in the seat across from him — the one Meach had occupied moments earlier — and raised her dress up over her head, exposing her red-lace bra and panties. Her fingertips pressed down on the plump lips of her pussy through the red fabric.

"You hungry?" she asked in a tone that was just a pinch over a whisper.

Blake did not hesitate.

He would have thrown the table to the side had it not been attached to the floor.

In a single motion, he swung her chair so that the foot of it was in the aisle, pushed her knees up by her ears, and put his nose and lips right on the crouch of her panties.

He shut his eyes and inhaled deeply.

If there was one tantalizing scent in the world that made his dick throb it was the always fresh scent of his wife's gushy nookie. It was sweeter than any candy and more potent than any Kush. He kissed and licked at the fabric before finally fingering it aside for a taste of the real goodies.

Alexus put her hands on his head as he took her clitoris in his mouth. He sucked it and swished saliva around it like he'd grown fond of doing, knowing without a doubt that it would drive her wild.

"You get me every...time like this," she moaned, and bit down on her lower lip. "Mmmmmmm...yeah, yeah..."

Blake dug a finger in her and went on sucking, his dick growing harder as the seconds passed. She saw his huge, straining, veiny erection and shut her eyes in anticipation of what it would feel like going in. It had been so long since they'd last made love. A part of her twisted mind thought that maybe he'd lost his mojo dealing with his side chicks. Maybe he wouldn't be able to perform the way he previously had. She thought back to their honeymoon, when he'd worn her out in bed in Ibiza, Spain.

"I want that honeymoon dick, baby," she said, holding the back of his head so that his face stayed mashed in her pussy. "You gon' give it to me?"

Blake could only nod. He went on sucking her clit until she tensed up a few minutes later. Then he moved aside and rapidly rubbed it as she squirted and trembled in orgasm, stroking his long member the entire time.

"You say you want that honeymoon dick?" he asked. "I'll give you that honeymoon dick."

Alexus couldn't stop shaking. She folded her arms under her legs and held them to the side as Blake lined up his dick for what would undoubtedly be a rough entry. She squeezed her eyes shut and gasped as he pushed the head in.

"I got that honeymoon dick right here for you." He eased forward, giving her an inch at a time. "This what you wanted, ain't it? Huh? Tell me it's what you wanted."

"It's what I wanted," she said.

"I didn't hear you, what was that?"

"It's what I wanted!" Alexus repeated, louder this time as Blake jammed in as many inches as her poor little nookie could take.

She whimpered and moaned and squirmed beneath him as he reminded her why she'd fallen in love with his sex game five years ago.

He fucked her like she owed him money and didn't want to pay up. He fucked her like he was raping her instead of the way she imagined a loving husband would do. There was no gentleness in his strokes, just a carnal pounding that brought tears to her eyes.

She almost yelled for him to stop. His dick was too big, so long and thick that it hurt every time he dunked it into her. But it was a good hurt, a pain that she'd much rather endure than run away from. It was the kind of pain that a girl loved and wanted again when it was over, the kind she'd have to run and tell her friends about on a later date.

She found herself squirting in orgasm for the second time in less than five minutes. Blake held her knees in his strong hands and never slowed his steady, powerful thrusts. What he was doing was the definition of "beating up the pussy", and he knew it. It was written all over his face.

Alexus tried not to think of whether or not he'd been doing Bubbles, Nona, and Barbie the same way over the past few months. Instead she looked at the big yellow diamond ring on her finger and reminded herself that Blake King was her husband. He wasn't married to those other bitches; he was hers.

The painful strokes seemed to last forever and a day. When Alexus could no longer take it, she pushed him off her and curled up in the seat with her knees to her chest, looking at him like he'd just sexually assaulted her.

He grinned, stroking. "What? I thought you said you wanted that honeymoon dick?"

"I'll be dead before I even get to see Gamuza if we keep this up," she said breathlessly. "You're trying to kill me. I know it. You're trying to kill me for going after your sluts."

Blake put his hands on the seat's armrests and leaned in for a kiss. "Come on, baby, let me finish. Turn around. I'll hit it from the back. It won't hurt as much."

"Yeah, right. It's too fucking big, Blake. It's going to hurt no matter what position we're in."

"No, it won't, I'm telling you," he insisted.

"You're telling me whatever you need to tell me to keep brutalizing my kitty," Alexus countered, but she turned her back to him anyway and raised her ass up in the air. "Hurry up."

He lined up the crown of his dick with her slick opening and impaled her without a second thought.

Alexus was sucking in a lungful of air when she noticed that Blake had set his phones down on the table. She briefly considered snatching them and running off to the bathroom, but his hands went to her waist and he started slamming in and out of her, and the idea quickly left her.

"You don't know how much I missed this," Blake said between breaths. He rubbed the palms of his hands down the arch of her back as he continued his heartless thrusts.

She crawled down from the chair in a thinly veiled attempt to get away from him, but he was on her like a lion. When they got to the floor, he pushed her flat on her stomach and put his full weight on her as he went right back to pounding.

She came again. This time she screamed out in ecstasy, moaning louder than she ever had, and she hoped that the others standing outside on the tarmac didn't hear her. Her pussy made sopping wet noises on Blake's monster pipe. He coiled her hair around his fist and lightly sank his teeth into her shoulder. The bite turned into a suction.

"I love yoooooou," Alexus moaned, stretching out the last word. There were tears of painful joy in her eyes. Now she knew the meaning behind the saying 'It hurts so good', because that was the only way to explain the feeling of Blake's oversized penis stretching out her nookie.

She felt a sharp exhalation of breath on the back of her neck as Blake stiffened. She felt his dick twitching around inside her. She felt him firing off rope after rope of gunky protein babies.

He lay on her for a few seconds afterward, breathing hard on her shoulder. His dick went limp inside her.

"That was definitely...that honeymoon dick," Alexus managed to say between breaths.

Blake held himself up on his hands as she turned over on her back. He kissed her.

"I love you so much, Blake. I really do," Alexus said, caressing the side of his face. "I know I can get a little crazy sometimes but it's only because of how much I love you. If you would only fuck with me and me only things would be okay."

"Didn't I tell you I was done with those other women?" He looked so handsome and convincing.

Alexus rolled her eyes skeptically. "Pardon me for not believing you. You've fucked a hundred bitches already, and I'm willing to bet that the hundred and first Dalmatian bitch isn't far from your list of bitches to visit."

Blake stood and pulled on his boxers and jeans. Sitting up on the polished mahogany floor, Alexus looked up at him.

"Okay," she said, "I'll make you a promise right now that I swear to never go against. If you can change your phone numbers and leave those bitches alone, I swear on our son's life that I'll let them live."

"Why'd you kill Danielle? She didn't have nothing to do with them. I never fucked her."

"Yeah, you hadn't fucked her yet. You wanted to. I saw the way you looked at her. Plus, her friend is the bitch you had a baby by, so fuck her and fuck you for taking up for the bitch."

Blake chuckled and shook his head.

Alexus felt her anger returning. She got up and put the dress back on. "Don't laugh at me, Blake. I'm dead fucking serious. I'm not trying to get mad, okay? Just listen to me."

"I'm listening." He was picking up his duffle bag. "I'm with you, baby." He walked over to her and gave her a kiss. "I'm here, a'ight? Ain't going nowhere. You're my wife and the mother of my son. We've been together this long, might as well try and make it work. Just stop sending people to kill my exes. That ain't gon' do nothin' but push me away."

"That's not what I'm trying to do." Alexus became emotional. She hugged him, and tears filled her eyes, only these were tears of uncertainty. Her heart swelled up with an emotion she couldn't name. She was a young woman married to the love of her life, and the fear of losing him was heartbreaking. "Just...please...stay with me," she said.

Blake kissed her on the forehead. "I'm here forever, baby. Now let's get to this show and catch up with that old ass nigga Gamuza."

Chapter 39

A heavy pall of weed smoke hung over the crowd of over 95,000 men and women who'd come to Estadio Azteca (the Aztec Stadium). Bulletface hadn't expected so many Americans to be present, but there were many. He was surprised to see Joya, his uncle Noble's daughter, waving her hands in the air in front of the stage as he emerged from behind the gold stage curtain wearing a Louis Vuitton bulletproof vest over brand-new black Balmain jeans and started rapping "I'm Ready", a song he'd collaborated on with P.A.T., his MBM rap artist who'd been shot and killed in Atlanta.

He was only half focused on the song he was performing.

The threat of the Zeta's boss possibly being present in the building had him on high alert.

He scanned the crowd as he rapped.

There weren't many older people, and certainly no 90-something year olds. Mostly everyone looked to be in their early twenties to late thirties. He spotted a few celebs in the front near his little cousin. One older white man with a receding hairline wore a tight black T-shirt with the word SECURITY stenciled across its chest and back, but he wasn't old enough to be Gamuza.

The second song Bulletface was due to perform called for more focus. It was "DBG", a track he'd recently recorded with Meach. He had a hard time remembering the words to the song but he did his best.

'DBG, we dem bad guys, Money Bag guys, stay mad high
And we eatin' like fat guys, hit the strip club lettin' cash fly
Sneak diss and I'ma let the Mac fly
Bleed em out, no tampons
Bulletface, got long straps for the opps, they can get clapped on
Jewelry flash like lights, guns flash camera, fuck it scream action
I bought two K's when you got one, hun'ed shots in the damn drum

Last nigga that ran up got blammed up with that damn gun
Bananas, bananas, I'm ridin' round wit' bananas
Catch you late night, let it bang bang, shoot a nigga out his
pajamas...'

Surprisingly — or perhaps unsurprisingly, since he freestyled
all his raps — Bulletface was able to remember the beginning lyrics,
and the rest came out naturally.

Just as Meach began his verse, Blake noticed a little old lady
in a wheelchair sitting in front of the stage.

She hadn't been there minutes prior.

Blake looked back to where Enrique was standing with a group
of Costilla Cartel soldiers disguised as security. He gave Enrique
the signal. Maybe Gamuza had come out dressed as an elderly
woman. He wouldn't need to do much trying on the elderly part.

As it turned out, though, the old woman was just an old
woman, brought to the concert by her sister who'd somehow mis-
taken Bulletface for Pit Bull.

Alexus's men swept through the crowd in search of Gamuza,
but unfortunately the Zeta cartel boss was nowhere to be found.

Blake was actually quite happy that Gamuza hadn't shown his
face. What Blake wanted ultimately was peace, and he was deter-
mined to get it, even if it meant getting as far away from his maniacal wife as possible.

After the show, he went backstage and found Alexus sitting in
a chair along the hallway wall. She looked up at him with a disap-
pointed expression on her heavenly brown face.

"I just knew it would work," she muttered. "What was I thinking? Like he would show his face here, knowing I'd more than
likely be here with you."

"It's all good, baby." Blake grinned as she stood up and rested
her forearms on his shoulders. She gazed into his eyes, worried.
"Don't look all sad like that. Forget about Gamuza. Let's focus on
gettin' this bread and taking care of the kids. That's all I'm tryna
do, a'ight? You with me?"

She nodded her head and hugged him for a long moment.

Unbeknownst to her, Blake had already given his pilot strict orders on where to go once he returned to the airport, and sadly, being with Alexus wasn't part of the plan.

King Rio

Chapter 40

"Blake, do you really believe this'll work?"

"It'll definitely work. Have faith in me."

"I don't know..." Nona shook her head timidly.

Instead of Spain Blake had chosen to vacation in Honolulu, Hawaii. He'd left the kids with Rita and Alexus, but there was no keeping him in Mexico. He'd changed his phone numbers and hadn't given them to anyone but Nona, Bubbles, and his MBM artists, making them all promise not to give the numbers to Alexus.

He and Nona were reclined in lounge chairs on a strip of private beach behind the oceanfront, ten-million-dollar home he'd rented just for the two of them. She had her Kindle computer tablet in hand, reading a book by a girl she'd met on Facebook named Nako.

Blake, on the other hand, was sipping his usual cup of iced Lean. He'd hired ten new bodyguards to keep the fans away; his old bodyguards had been Costilla Cartel militants, and he didn't want anything to do with them, either.

Further down the shoreline, men and women with cameras were busy snapping long-distance pictures of him and Nona.

Somehow, they'd gotten word that Bulletface was on the island.

"Those pictures are going to end up on TMZ," Nona said, putting on her Chanel sunglasses. "Dish Nation, too. This may not be the best place to hide out from—"

"I'm not hiding," Blake said. "I'm just done with her. I'm getting a divorce. That's all there is to it."

He was feeling himself a bit more than usual today. His Louis Vuitton sandals and swimming trunks might have had something to do with it. He always enjoyed himself whenever those famous LV logos were plastered all over his clothing.

His smile brightened as one of his iPhones started ringing. "It's Bubbles," he said showing the phone screen to Nona before he swiped his thumb across it to answer the call.

"What up, big booty?" he said, his voice replete with cheer.

"You sneaky little fucker."
Blake's mouth fell agape.
Wide-eyed, he turned to Nona.
The voice he'd just heard belonged to none other than Alexus Costilla.

To Be Continued…
The Cocaine Princess 10
Coming Soon

Lock Down Publications and Ca$h Presents assisted
publishing packages.

BASIC PACKAGE $499
Editing
Cover Design
Formatting

UPGRADED PACKAGE $800
Typing
Editing
Cover Design
Formatting

ADVANCE PACKAGE $1,200
Typing
Editing
Cover Design
Formatting
Copyright registration
Proofreading
Upload book to Amazon

LDP SUPREME PACKAGE $1,500
Typing
Editing
Cover Design
Formatting
Copyright registration
Proofreading
Set up Amazon account
Upload book to Amazon
Advertise on LDP Amazon and Facebook page

***Other services available upon request. Additional charges may apply
Lock Down Publications
P.O. Box 944
Stockbridge, GA 30281-9998
Phone # 470 303-9761

Submission Guideline

Submit the first three chapters of your completed manuscript to ldpsubmissions@gmail.com, subject line: Your book's title. The manuscript must be in a .doc file and sent as an attachment. Document should be in Times New Roman, double spaced and in size 12 font. Also, provide your synopsis and full contact information. If sending multiple submissions, they must each be in a separate email.

Have a story but no way to send it electronically? You can still submit to LDP/Ca$h Presents. Send in the first three chapters, written or typed, of your completed manuscript to:

LDP: Submissions Dept
Po Box 944
Stockbridge, Ga 30281

DO NOT send original manuscript. Must be a duplicate.

Provide your synopsis and a cover letter containing your full contact information.

Thanks for considering LDP and Ca$h Presents.

NEW RELEASES

IT'S JUST ME AND YOU 2 by AH'MILLION

SOUL OF A HUSTLER, HEART OF A KILLER 3 by
SAYNOMORE

THE COCAINE PRINCESS 9 by KING RIO

Coming Soon from Lock Down Publications/Ca$h Presents

BLOOD OF A BOSS VI

SHADOWS OF THE GAME II

TRAP BASTARD II

By **Askari**

LOYAL TO THE GAME **IV**

By **T.J. & Jelissa**

TRUE SAVAGE **VIII**

MIDNIGHT CARTEL IV

DOPE BOY MAGIC IV

CITY OF KINGZ III

NIGHTMARE ON SILENT AVE II

THE PLUG OF LIL MEXICO II

CLASSIC CITY II

By **Chris Green**

BLAST FOR ME **III**

A SAVAGE DOPEBOY III

CUTTHROAT MAFIA III

DUFFLE BAG CARTEL VII

HEARTLESS GOON VI

By **Ghost**

A HUSTLER'S DECEIT III

KILL ZONE II

BAE BELONGS TO ME III

TIL DEATH II

By **Aryanna**

KING OF THE TRAP III

By **T.J. Edwards**

GORILLAZ IN THE BAY V

3X KRAZY III

STRAIGHT BEAST MODE III
De'Kari
KINGPIN KILLAZ IV
STREET KINGS III
PAID IN BLOOD III
CARTEL KILLAZ IV
DOPE GODS III
Hood Rich
SINS OF A HUSTLA II
ASAD
YAYO V
Bred In The Game 2
S. Allen
THE STREETS WILL TALK II
By Yolanda Moore
SON OF A DOPE FIEND III
HEAVEN GOT A GHETTO III
SKI MASK MONEY III
By Renta
LOYALTY AIN'T PROMISED III
By Keith Williams
I'M NOTHING WITHOUT HIS LOVE II
SINS OF A THUG II
TO THE THUG I LOVED BEFORE II
IN A HUSTLER I TRUST II
By Monet Dragun
QUIET MONEY IV
EXTENDED CLIP III
THUG LIFE IV
By **Trai'Quan**

THE STREETS MADE ME IV

By **Larry D. Wright**

IF YOU CROSS ME ONCE III

ANGEL V

By **Anthony Fields**

THE STREETS WILL NEVER CLOSE IV

By **K'ajji**

HARD AND RUTHLESS III

KILLA KOUNTY IV

By **Khufu**

MONEY GAME III

By **Smoove Dolla**

JACK BOYS VS DOPE BOYS IV

A GANGSTA'S QUR'AN V

COKE GIRLZ II

COKE BOYS II

LIFE OF A SAVAGE V

CHI'RAQ GANGSTAS V

SOSA GANG IV

BRONX SAVAGES II

BODYMORE KINGPINS II

BLOOD OF A GOON II

By **Romell Tukes**

MURDA WAS THE CASE III

Elijah R. Freeman

AN UNFORESEEN LOVE IV

BABY, I'M WINTERTIME COLD III

By **Meesha**

QUEEN OF THE ZOO III

King Rio

By **Black Migo**
CONFESSIONS OF A JACKBOY III
By Nicholas Lock
KING KILLA II
By Vincent "Vitto" Holloway
BETRAYAL OF A THUG III
By Fre$h
THE BIRTH OF A GANGSTER III
By Delmont Player
TREAL LOVE II
By Le'Monica Jackson
FOR THE LOVE OF BLOOD III
By Jamel Mitchell
RAN OFF ON DA PLUG II
By Paper Boi Rari
HOOD CONSIGLIERE III
By Keese
PRETTY GIRLS DO NASTY THINGS II
By Nicole Goosby
LOVE IN THE TRENCHES II
By Corey Robinson
FOREVER GANGSTA III
By Adrian Dulan
THE COCAINE PRINCESS X
SUPER GREMLIN II
By King Rio
CRIME BOSS II
Playa Ray
LOYALTY IS EVERYTHING III
Molotti

202

The Cocaine Princess

HERE TODAY GONE TOMORROW II
By Fly Rock
REAL G'S MOVE IN SILENCE II
By Von Diesel
GRIMEY WAYS IV
By Ray Vinci
SALUTE MY SAVAGERY II
By Fumiya Payne
BLOOD AND GAMES II
By King Dream

Available Now

RESTRAINING ORDER **I & II**
By **CA$H & Coffee**
LOVE KNOWS NO BOUNDARIES **I II & III**
By **Coffee**
RAISED AS A GOON I, II, III & IV
BRED BY THE SLUMS I, II, III
BLAST FOR ME I & II
ROTTEN TO THE CORE I II III
A BRONX TALE I, II, III
DUFFLE BAG CARTEL I II III IV V VI
HEARTLESS GOON I II III IV V
A SAVAGE DOPEBOY I II
DRUG LORDS I II III

CUTTHROAT MAFIA I II
KING OF THE TRENCHES
By **Ghost**
LAY IT DOWN **I & II**
LAST OF A DYING BREED I II
BLOOD STAINS OF A SHOTTA I & II III
By **Jamaica**
LOYAL TO THE GAME I II III
LIFE OF SIN I, II III
By **TJ & Jelissa**
BLOODY COMMAS I & II
SKI MASK CARTEL I II & III
KING OF NEW YORK I II,III IV V
RISE TO POWER I II III
COKE KINGS I II III IV V
BORN HEARTLESS I II III IV
KING OF THE TRAP I II
By **T.J. Edwards**
IF LOVING HIM IS WRONG…I & II
LOVE ME EVEN WHEN IT HURTS I II III
By **Jelissa**
WHEN THE STREETS CLAP BACK I & II III
THE HEART OF A SAVAGE I II III IV
MONEY MAFIA I II
LOYAL TO THE SOIL I II III
By **Jibril Williams**
A DISTINGUISHED THUG STOLE MY HEART I II & III
LOVE SHOULDN'T HURT I II III IV
RENEGADE BOYS I II III IV
PAID IN KARMA I II III

SAVAGE STORMS I II III
AN UNFORESEEN LOVE I II III
BABY, I'M WINTERTIME COLD I II
By **Meesha**
A GANGSTER'S CODE I &, II III
A GANGSTER'S SYN I II III
THE SAVAGE LIFE I II III
CHAINED TO THE STREETS I II III
BLOOD ON THE MONEY I II III
A GANGSTA'S PAIN I II III
By J-Blunt
PUSH IT TO THE LIMIT
By **Bre' Hayes**
BLOOD OF A BOSS **I, II, III, IV, V**
SHADOWS OF THE GAME
TRAP BASTARD
By **Askari**
THE STREETS BLEED MURDER **I, II & III**
THE HEART OF A GANGSTA I II& III
By **Jerry Jackson**
CUM FOR ME I II III IV V VI VII VIII
An **LDP Erotica Collaboration**
BRIDE OF A HUSTLA **I II & II**
THE FETTI GIRLS **I, II& III**
CORRUPTED BY A GANGSTA I, II III, IV
BLINDED BY HIS LOVE
THE PRICE YOU PAY FOR LOVE I, II ,III
DOPE GIRL MAGIC I II III
By **Destiny Skai**
WHEN A GOOD GIRL GOES BAD

King Rio

By **Adrienne**
THE COST OF LOYALTY I II III
By **Kweli**
A GANGSTER'S REVENGE **I II III & IV**
THE BOSS MAN'S DAUGHTERS I II III IV V
A SAVAGE LOVE **I & II**
BAE BELONGS TO ME I II
A HUSTLER'S DECEIT I, II, III
WHAT BAD BITCHES DO I, II, III
SOUL OF A MONSTER I II III
KILL ZONE
A DOPE BOY'S QUEEN I II III
TIL DEATH
By **Aryanna**
A KINGPIN'S AMBITON
A KINGPIN'S AMBITION **II**
I MURDER FOR THE DOUGH
By **Ambitious**
TRUE SAVAGE I II III IV V VI VII
DOPE BOY MAGIC I, II, III
MIDNIGHT CARTEL I II III
CITY OF KINGZ I II
NIGHTMARE ON SILENT AVE
THE PLUG OF LIL MEXICO II
CLASSIC CITY
By **Chris Green**
A DOPEBOY'S PRAYER
By **Eddie "Wolf" Lee**
THE KING CARTEL **I, II & III**
By **Frank Gresham**

THESE NIGGAS AIN'T LOYAL **I, II & III**

By **Nikki Tee**

GANGSTA SHYT **I II &III**

By **CATO**

THE ULTIMATE BETRAYAL

By **Phoenix**

BOSS'N UP **I , II & III**

By **Royal Nicole**

I LOVE YOU TO DEATH

By **Destiny J**

I RIDE FOR MY HITTA

I STILL RIDE FOR MY HITTA

By **Misty Holt**

LOVE & CHASIN' PAPER

By **Qay Crockett**

TO DIE IN VAIN

SINS OF A HUSTLA

By **ASAD**

BROOKLYN HUSTLAZ

By **Boogsy Morina**

BROOKLYN ON LOCK I & II

By **Sonovia**

GANGSTA CITY

By **Teddy Duke**

A DRUG KING AND HIS DIAMOND I & II III

A DOPEMAN'S RICHES

HER MAN, MINE'S TOO I, II

CASH MONEY HO'S

THE WIFEY I USED TO BE I II

PRETTY GIRLS DO NASTY THINGS

By Nicole Goosby
TRAPHOUSE KING **I II & III**
KINGPIN KILLAZ I II III
STREET KINGS I II
PAID IN BLOOD **I II**
CARTEL KILLAZ I II III
DOPE GODS I II
By **Hood Rich**
LIPSTICK KILLAH **I, II, III**
CRIME OF PASSION I II & III
FRIEND OR FOE I II III
By **Mimi**
STEADY MOBBN' **I, II, III**
THE STREETS STAINED MY SOUL I II III
By **Marcellus Allen**
WHO SHOT YA **I, II, III**
SON OF A DOPE FIEND I II
HEAVEN GOT A GHETTO I II
SKI MASK MONEY I II
Renta
GORILLAZ IN THE BAY **I II III IV**
TEARS OF A GANGSTA I II
3X KRAZY I II
STRAIGHT BEAST MODE I II
DE'KARI
TRIGGADALE I II III
MURDAROBER WAS THE CASE I II
Elijah R. Freeman
GOD BLESS THE TRAPPERS I, II, III
THESE SCANDALOUS STREETS I, II, III

FEAR MY GANGSTA I, II, III IV, V
THESE STREETS DON'T LOVE NOBODY I, II
BURY ME A G I, II, III, IV, V
A GANGSTA'S EMPIRE I, II, III, IV
THE DOPEMAN'S BODYGAURD I II
THE REALEST KILLAZ I II III
THE LAST OF THE OGS I II III
Tranay Adams
THE STREETS ARE CALLING
Duquie Wilson
MARRIED TO A BOSS I II III
By Destiny Skai & Chris Green
KINGZ OF THE GAME I II III IV V VI VII
CRIME BOSS
Playa Ray
SLAUGHTER GANG I II III
RUTHLESS HEART I II III
By Willie Slaughter
FUK SHYT
By Blakk Diamond
DON'T F#CK WITH MY HEART I II
By Linnea
ADDICTED TO THE DRAMA I II III
IN THE ARM OF HIS BOSS II
By Jamila
YAYO I II III IV
A SHOOTER'S AMBITION I II
BRED IN THE GAME
By S. Allen
TRAP GOD I II III

King Rio

RICH $AVAGE I II III
MONEY IN THE GRAVE I II III
By Martell Troublesome Bolden
FOREVER GANGSTA I II
GLOCKS ON SATIN SHEETS I II
By Adrian Dulan
TOE TAGZ I II III IV
LEVELS TO THIS SHYT I II
IT'S JUST ME AND YOU I II
By Ah'Million
KINGPIN DREAMS I II III
RAN OFF ON DA PLUG
By Paper Boi Rari
CONFESSIONS OF A GANGSTA I II III IV
CONFESSIONS OF A JACKBOY I II
By Nicholas Lock
I'M NOTHING WITHOUT HIS LOVE
SINS OF A THUG
TO THE THUG I LOVED BEFORE
A GANGSTA SAVED XMAS
IN A HUSTLER I TRUST
By Monet Dragun
CAUGHT UP IN THE LIFE I II III
THE STREETS NEVER LET GO I II III
By Robert Baptiste
NEW TO THE GAME I II III
MONEY, MURDER & MEMORIES I II III
By **Malik D. Rice**
LIFE OF A SAVAGE I II III IV
A GANGSTA'S QUR'AN I II III IV

The Cocaine Princess

MURDA SEASON I II III

GANGLAND CARTEL I II III

CHI'RAQ GANGSTAS I II III IV

KILLERS ON ELM STREET I II III

JACK BOYZ N DA BRONX I II III

A DOPEBOY'S DREAM I II III

JACK BOYS VS DOPE BOYS I II III

COKE GIRLZ

COKE BOYS

SOSA GANG I II III

BRONX SAVAGES

BODYMORE KINGPINS

BLOOD OF A GOON

By Romell Tukes

LOYALTY AIN'T PROMISED I II

By Keith Williams

QUIET MONEY I II III

THUG LIFE I II III

EXTENDED CLIP I II

A GANGSTA'S PARADISE

By **Trai'Quan**

THE STREETS MADE ME I II III

By **Larry D. Wright**

THE ULTIMATE SACRIFICE I, II, III, IV, V, VI

KHADIFI

IF YOU CROSS ME ONCE I II

ANGEL I II III IV

IN THE BLINK OF AN EYE

By **Anthony Fields**

THE LIFE OF A HOOD STAR

211

By Ca$h & Rashia Wilson

THE STREETS WILL NEVER CLOSE I II III

By K'ajji

CREAM I II III

THE STREETS WILL TALK

By Yolanda Moore

NIGHTMARES OF A HUSTLA I II III

BLOOD AND GAMES

By King Dream

CONCRETE KILLA I II III

VICIOUS LOYALTY I II III

By Kingpen

HARD AND RUTHLESS I II

MOB TOWN 251

THE BILLIONAIRE BENTLEYS I II III

REAL G'S MOVE IN SILENCE

By Von Diesel

GHOST MOB

Stilloan Robinson

MOB TIES I II III IV V VI

SOUL OF A HUSTLER, HEART OF A KILLER I II III

GORILLAZ IN THE TRENCHES I II III

By SayNoMore

BODYMORE MURDERLAND I II III

THE BIRTH OF A GANGSTER I II

By Delmont Player

FOR THE LOVE OF A BOSS

By C. D. Blue

MOBBED UP I II III IV

THE BRICK MAN I II III IV V

THE COCAINE PRINCESS I II III IV V VI VII VIII IX

SUPER GREMLIN

By King Rio

KILLA KOUNTY I II III IV

By Khufu

MONEY GAME I II

By Smoove Dolla

A GANGSTA'S KARMA I II III

By FLAME

KING OF THE TRENCHES I II III

by **GHOST & TRANAY ADAMS**

QUEEN OF THE ZOO I II

By **Black Migo**

GRIMEY WAYS I II III

By Ray Vinci

XMAS WITH AN ATL SHOOTER

By Ca$h & Destiny Skai

KING KILLA

By Vincent "Vitto" Holloway

BETRAYAL OF A THUG I II

By Fre$h

THE MURDER QUEENS I II III

By Michael Gallon

TREAL LOVE

By Le'Monica Jackson

FOR THE LOVE OF BLOOD I II

By Jamel Mitchell

HOOD CONSIGLIERE I II

By Keese

PROTÉGÉ OF A LEGEND I II III

LOVE IN THE TRENCHES

By Corey Robinson

BORN IN THE GRAVE I II III

By Self Made Tay

MOAN IN MY MOUTH

By XTASY

TORN BETWEEN A GANGSTER AND A GENTLEMAN

By J-BLUNT & Miss Kim

LOYALTY IS EVERYTHING I II

Molotti

HERE TODAY GONE TOMORROW

By Fly Rock

PILLOW PRINCESS

By S. Hawkins

NAÏVE TO THE STREETS

WOMEN LIE MEN LIE I II III

GIRLS FALL LIKE DOMINOS

STACK BEFORE YOU SPURLGE

FIFTY SHADES OF SNOW I II III

By A. Roy Milligan

SALUTE MY SAVAGERY

By Fumiya Payne

BOOKS BY LDP'S CEO, CA$H

TRUST IN NO MAN

TRUST IN NO MAN 2

TRUST IN NO MAN 3

BONDED BY BLOOD

SHORTY GOT A THUG

THUGS CRY

THUGS CRY 2

THUGS CRY 3

TRUST NO BITCH

TRUST NO BITCH 2

TRUST NO BITCH 3

TIL MY CASKET DROPS

RESTRAINING ORDER

RESTRAINING ORDER 2

IN LOVE WITH A CONVICT

LIFE OF A HOOD STAR

XMAS WITH AN ATL SHOOTER

King Rio